Frank Hickey
Baxston Resident
and
L.A.P.D. Retired

Funny Bunny Hunts the Horn Bug

To Chris
With respect
and affection

BY THE SAME AUTHOR

BOOKS

The Gypsy Twist

FEATURE FILMS

Spy, The Movie
(co-written with Charles Messina
& Lynwood Shiva Sawyer)

Funny Bunny Hunts the Horn Bug

A Max Royster Mystery

by Frank Hickey

Library of Congress
Catalogue-in-Publication Data

Funny Bunny Hunts the Horn Bug / Frank Hickey
1. Fiction - Crime 2. Fiction - Mystery 3. Fiction - Hardboiled

Published by Pigtown Books

ISBN: 978-0-9848810-1-7

For further information, please contact:

info@pigtownbooks.com

10 9 8 7 6 5 4 3 2 1

First Edition / First Issue

To Jean Hogan Hickey

1923-2007

Johnny Weissmuller Water Show Dancer,
Copacabana Dancer, Broadway Actress,
Member: Pax Christi and The Catholic Worker

PROLOGUE

Greenwich Village was a carnival of springtime magic whirling and laughing around the dance floor and my partner.

"Dancing is magic," I reminded her.

"Max, you say that every time."

"Because it becomes more true," I said.

Aline showed a classic face with delicate dark brows and eyes. A lime-green summer dress moved with our rumba. She smelled of cinnamon from the cappuccino she was drinking.

Other couples danced past me. Their flanks said that I was slow.

The mirror behind us reflected me as a thick redhead, crowding fifty and weighing too much. For dancing, I always wore black. Alongside Aline's freshness, my cowboy moustache made me look sinister.

On stage, the Cuban singer crooned "Sabor A Mi."

Through an open window, I heard a man's voice from the street outside.

My green eyes asked, "What the hell?"

"Ow, goddamnit!" the man said, near panic. "Are you crazy?"

His tone raised my hackles.

"You cut me!" he said.

"Give that wallet!" a woman spat. "Or I cut you more."

I broke away from the startled Aline.

"Family emergency," I said. "Just remembered. I'll be back later."

"Why don't you grow up and get organized like other men?" she asked.

Aline did not know my job.

She spun and snagged another partner.

I went bounding through the fire doors then down a flight to the street. The stairs hurt my feet. The staircase smelled of cigar smoke.

I burst through the steel door onto the street.

Twenty feet away, a stagey blonde woman stood over a moaning black man on the sidewalk. Wet blood dappled the sidewalk and her right hand. Her shoes scraped the sidewalk.

"Police Officer!" I bellowed. "Don't move!"

I never carried at a dance. My Glock and my nickeled police shield lay back in my apartment.

"Officer!" the man said. "She cut me!"

"He tried raping me!" she said. "You know how they are."

"Sure thing," I said. "Always chasing you blondes. That's why I heard you ask for cash. You're under arrest."

She lunged at me.

Something metal in her hand slashed at me.

I leaned back, kicked high and felt my foot kick her arm near the elbow. She cussed. Her hand opened. The wet razor blade pinwheeled from her fingers, catching streetlight.

The blade dropped somewhere dark.

But she rushed me.

She was a strong built woman about 30. As a street hustler, she knew everything about men's bodies. She knew how to fight and take them apart.

Nerves shook my hands.

She threw strikes. I smelled a sweet perfume and felt knuckles BOOM! my face. Then garbage smell choked me.

I was on the ground. Her shoes clattered away.

She loped across Second Avenue. Traffic screamed and lurched to stops.

Then she ran west on Seventh Street.

Somehow, I carried my beef behind her, panting like a hippo getting into hot water.

"What's up, dude?" a skateboarder asked, slouching at my elbow, cap on sideways.

"You are, Skates," I said. "Police. Can you skate to that corner on Seventh and Ale Place in thirty seconds?"

"Twenty."

"A blonde woman, 30, big-boned, black dress. Don't let her leave."

"I'm deputized?"

"With all my authority," I said.

Skates whooped. He bang-slam-crashed his skateboard along Seventh.

I cellphoned 911.

My voice shook as I gave the operator all the up-to-the-minute news.

Skates reached the corner near Ale Place. Accordion music mixed with guffaws from inside McSorley's. He stood about 90 feet from me. Nobody could get past him.

"The perp is locked down on East Seventh between Ale Place and Two Avenue," I sputtered into my phone. "There are about five stores open on the block now. And about nine apartment buildings opening onto this block."

"We got units en route," the 911 operator said. "You say that you're off-duty. Just remember that, officer."

"You're talking to the right man," I said "And here comes your victim. Roll me an ambulance here."

The man who had been flat on the sidewalk tottered across Second Avenue. Blood streamed down his face. It dripped off his jawbone onto his jolly polo shirt.

"She gave me a scar," he blubbered. "I'm going to have a scar!"

"What's the deal here?"

"Man, I don't want to talk to you. You let her slide!"

Looking at him now, I could see that he was younger than be had looked before. He might be 22, with a fullback's build and smooth looks, unmarked before tonight.

"Talk, anyway," I said. "I'm all that you got."

"What do you care? Huh? We started rapping on the subway. Just friendly, you know. She's older than me but seemed interested. Said I had a great body."

"God bless her."

"I mean, oldsters need sex, too," he said.

"So I hear."

"Then we leave the subway together. Somehow she started kissing and feeling me up. I went with it. Then she asked for money. I started pulling away and she cut me with something. Now I'm scarred!"

"I'll help you. And I'll let you in on a secret. Women love scars."

No blonde woman showed on the street.

An NYPD blue-and-white car bulled down the avenue. The roof light bled cherry Christmas colors. The Driver Officer bumped the curb. His partner, the Recorder Officer, cussed.

"Hey, pal," the Recorder Officer said. "Whaddya got?"

"Max Royster, off-duty, Seven-One Precinct. I got Rob One, lady blonde perp up this block somewheres. Either in a store or some apartment vestibule. Put your next car up there on Ale Place to relieve that skateboarder kid."

The Recorder Officer made a face. He stood about three bulky inches over my six feet, pale-faced against limp brown hair and bent tin eyeglasses.

Tobacco smell blended with sweat as he leaned closer to me. Smile lines grooved his mouth but he was not smiling now.

"We can't do that," he said. "Where's your shield?"

"Back in my crib. Here's my ID."

The crumpled paper unfolded from my wallet. It showed the NYPD seal and my name and shield and command. It also said that I had lost three vacation days for working overtime without notifying the desk.

"That's no ID. It's just an official NYPD reprimand on PO Max Royster."

"Can you think of a better ID?"

"Royster, we had to Taser some PCP fool on this street. Then we did three Community Policing projects, to calm the silly whiners down. Anarchists. Career complainers. Letter-writers. So we can't search for this perp here. Everyone will get their nuts twisted if we search like you want."

I stepped back

"You're jerkin' my Gherkin," I said. "You can't be serious."

"Nope. Captain told us, leave this block alone."

"Community Policing, known to us cops as 'ComPol,' means getting closer to your beat by walking and talking," I said. "Helping with non-cop trouble. Developing relations with them. But it does NOT mean that we stop policing."

"Cap don't want to know," the Recorder said. "He pretty dumb."

"A real sharp cookie," the Driver said. She was a muscled type, the kind who does pull-ups without straining. A tattoo of a surfboard decorated her left wrist. Her left canine tooth winked gold.

"He'll punish us for shaking up this block," the Driver said. "Days off and craparoo assignments."

"But she cut this guy," I said. "And we can jail her where she belongs."

"Just a boy-girl cat fight," the Driver said. "He said-she said."

"So you can take off, pal," the Recorder said. "We got this covered."

My breath blew out.

I stepped towards the Recorder.

"You mean that you got this covered up," I said. "What about me? She hit a cop. Or doesn't ComPol care about that?"

"You shouldn't get involved off duty."

"Well, I am. Let's please call your sergeant."

"No," the Recorder said.

There it hung.

I cellphoned 911 line again to put it on tape. Emotions warbled my voice worse.

The street corner smelled of dead beer and garbage.

The Sergeant who showed up was a round saggy joker who would have looked comfortable behind a butcher's counter.

His mud-colored hair was breaking white over the temples and needed cutting. He seemed a defeated bureaucrat.

You could see it in the wary gray eyes, avoiding contact and saying that he wanted to retire early tomorrow morning.

"No deal, Sport," he said. "We spent weeks stroking this block with ComPol bull sessions. I'm not throwing that away for one whore swinging some steel."

"What matters to you?" I asked.

"You don't. Keeping that moron captain off me does. And look at your vic here. Do you see him going to court on this?"

"Yes."

"Well, I don't. He wants to tonight. But tomorrow, less and less. You know them. If we bother this block tonight, those same jerks that we stroked will write new complaint letters on me. It's not worth it."

"I want her arrested!" the cut victim said in his clear college voice. "And I'll go to court."

"You're drinking tonight and she's your girlfriend," the Sergeant croaked. "We had other cops check the block, sir. She's gone."

"You're lying," the cut victim said. "Anyone can see that."

The Sergeant closed his eyes.

"She's gone, sir," the Sergeant repeated.

"ComPol says so," the Recorder said.

"ComPol is great for lazy cops," I said. "A new excuse for doing nothing."

"You want a complaint?" the Sergeant asked. "Little written reprimand?"

"Sir, do you need an ambulance?" I asked the victim.

"What do you care?"

"Ambulance?" I asked.

"Not from you."

"Then I'll see you home in a cab," I said. "Maybe we'll take an adult beverage on the way."

Thirty feet away, the woman burst out of a doorway, blonde hair flying. Her face twisted and turned ugly.

"Don't move, officer," the Sergeant said to me. "That's an order! I'll have you fired for Insubordination."

I ducked my head and tensed my dancing leg muscles. They hurt. Everything hurt.

She saw us standing on the corner, grimaced and then laughed as she ran. It sounded like a bad smoker's cough, hacking and spitting. She dodged The Skateboard Kid on the corner and kept running. You could hear the laugh all up and down the street.

"She's laughing at us, Sarge," I said. "And at your Community Policing."

CHAPTER 1.

Heat had crinkled the dark blue shirt that NYPD cops call "the bag" until it glued to my flanks and rode piggyback on me. I was sponging my wet way past Manhattan brownstones where the city's elite lived.

"You knock over my papers, I kill you!" the Korean merchant flailed his wiry arms. Everything in him sharpened as he stepped onto my sidewalk.

"We didn't do nothing!" the pale whitefish grandmother wailed. Her blue eyes blazed under dyed gold hair. She marshaled someone who looked like her daughter and a pudgy granddaughter under her arm.

"Kill all you!"

Her offspring circled to the grocer's left like a street boxer, moving to his weaker side. The Korean noticed. A teargas sprayer showed in his fist.

My heart hammered like a runaway horse inside the bag.

A stylish woman in soft leather boots and tailored jeans stepped in front of me, shifting her handbag to a shoulder.

"Excuse me," I said. "Let me pass."

She looked through me with light-colored eyes.

"I need to get past you," I said.

"There's no hurry," she said, her accent refined at some tony private school.

She slung her handbag, blocked me again and then walked away.

"Think that one over," I said.

The grocer shouted some more.

"Shill-yeh hamnida!" I shouted back in Korean. "Kyung-chahl!" or "Police! Stop right there! Both of you!"

The grandmother whipped around. Her daughter kept circling.

"I said STOP!" I bellowed, putting all of my 210 pounds behind it.

Somehow it worked. That was one more time.

"Listen up," I said, winging it. "If I want someone to ignore me, I'll get married."

The instantly forming Manhattan crowd eddied on the sidewalk near us. You could smell a clove cigarette, rich perfume and somebody's fresh running shoes.

"My friends, could we clear the sidewalk here?" I asked.

"You clear it," someone said. "You're the cop."

"Upper-class revolt," I said. "The attack of the lacrosse players."

The grocer swung the tear gas sprayer at me. Another grocer bobbed up behind him, hands held to hit someone. They both looked wired enough to slug me. Their eyes said that they did not care anymore.

A teenage Latino messenger leaned his bike against a parking meter and watched. For him, this was better than free TV.

My feet twitched as I stepped back.

A dog walker, a regal-looking man in a Madras suit and bowtie, walked by with a borzoi, a Russian wolfhound. The dog stretched out the leash, striking my thigh and stopping me from moving.

"Excuse me," I asked the dog walker. "Could you let me pass?"

He sniffed and ignored me.

The borzoi paid me more respect. He skittered out of the way.

My hand stopped the grocer with the tear gas.

"Put that tear gas in your pocket," I said. "Or I'll arrest you and end this little comedy right now."

He obeyed, cussing in Korean with what sounded like terrible words.

"Don't listen to him!" the dog walker said. "Call for his sergeant to come here. These police are getting out of hand."

I gave the dog walker my best subway glare.

"You, sir," I said to the grocer, "Do you pay taxes?"

"Too much taxes!"

"Well, I'm what you get for them. So let me earn them. Go back inside your store, handle your customers, and you and I will talk."

"They attack my store, my property!"

"That's why I'm here," I said. My hands shook, so I folded them across my Sam Browne gunbelt. "Both sides get to explain to me what happened. Then I punish, okay?"

"That's not fair!" the grandmother said. Her pink cheeks shook as she wagged her head.

"You'll be happy with what happens, I promise you," I said. "But I can't do anything until you talk to me. You, nobody else. Nobody is leaving, okay? How does that sound to you?"

"Like a grand mess!"

"Are you angry at me?" I asked.

"He has no right. Does he –"

"Are you low rent people?" I asked. "How old is that child? Do you want her to see all this? Would you rather speak to me privately?"

"Why you asking these questions?"

"What is your name?" I asked.

"Why?"

"My name's Max," I said. "What may I call you?"

My questions slowed her. They sometimes worked that way.

"Why do you want to know my name?"

"Well," I made her slow down even more. "Why not? Have you done anything wrong?"

"No!"

"Then, please, tell me."

Now I pitched my voice so low against the traffic noise that she had to strain to hear me. Some of the sidewalkers pooled away from us. That brought my breath back to me.

"My name is Mrs. Rhonda Klepfer," she said.

"That's fine, Mrs. Klepfer," I was almost whispering now and drawing out the words. "I want to thank you for helping me here today."

"This ain't a luncheon, Mama!" the daughter shouted. "He trying to flimflam you!"

I breathed out and shook my head slowly.

The daughter was thicker than I was, about five-feet-nine, and looked like one of life's losers, running in place to nowhere fast. They both appeared to be neighborhood loudmouths from Long Island, the kind that hate and avoid the city.

"He's just getting you off the track!" the daughter shouted.

I turned to the daughter, blading my body so that the gun stayed far from her.

"And what might be your name, young lady?" I asked.

My voice cracked. This was tearing me down and taking me apart.

"I don't have to tell you my name unless you get me a lawyer!"

"You're pretty sharp," I said. "Too much for me, anyway."

"By accident, right?" the daughter said. "Just an accident, you know, we knocked over this Chinese fool's newspapers. But I'm gonna come back and sue his ass."

"Let me handle this for you. Do you have a cellphone?"

"Why?"

This might work out for me, I thought.

"Now I know that nobody hit anyone," I said. "I will contact you later and tell you how I cited this man inside for Disorderly Conduct. But I can't do that without your phone number."

The daughter reluctantly gave me her digits.

"He has no right to cause this kind of scene," I continued. "How does that sound to you?"

The grandmother glared at the store. "He scared my little girl!"

"You are right," I lied, giving her the magic phrase. "That's where the Disorderly Conduct comes in. I'll be in touch, Mrs. Klepfer."

"You better not be lying to me! I got your name off your plate there. Royster, right?"

"Max Royster, yes, Mrs. Klepfer. Patrol Borough Manhattan North."

"You lie to me and I call Internal Affairs. Nobody trusts you cops now. That's why they pay you just 25K. Only slobs need apply."

"Thank you again, Mrs. Klepfer."

She shrugged and tugged the latest two generations with her back onto Madison Avenue.

"They're gone," I told the grocer. "If they come back, call 911. And don't wave that tear gas around again."

"This is my store!"

"This is my rule," I said. "As of today. If I see you threaten a child with gas, I'll cuff you and put you in jail."

I spun the handcuffs out of the case and thumped them on the counter.

"Clear enough?" I asked.

Outside, I tried taking a deep breath and hoping that my pulse would slow down.

"Man, that was sweet," the Latino messenger said. Gold inlays dotted his teeth under a scraggly moustache. "You gave that lady some verbal judo, right?"

"Gave her something."

"Man, you like to walk, don't you? I seen you up on 86th Street two hours ago."

"New world," I said. "Today's my first day working this kind of rich upper-class precinct. I call it 'The Playpen' where the rich never grow up."

"Yeah, you right about that."

"Back in Brooklyn, I'm used to my slum precinct where everyone needs cops. I live near this Playpen. But patrolling in the blue is different."

"They don't think they need you here, bro. Crime is down way low. And nobody respects New York cops anymore. Scandals, shootings and that 25,000 chump change they pay you."

"That's just twisted thinking," I said. "Every place needs cops protecting it."

"Sure as spit, bro. Give you an example. While you were talking that stank ho down, this dude was checking all the doors on the block. When he saw you, he took off. But he was trying to get inside some house there,"

I swiveled on my heels and looked back at the block of brownstones going up to Fifth Avenue.

"Do you see him now?" I asked.

"Naw. You scared him off."

"Which house?"

"Man, don't you listen? All of them. He went down the steps and tried the cellar doors, too."

"I appreciate the heads-up," I said. "My name's Max. What's yours?"

"Raymundo."

"Raymundo, what did this fool look like?"

"Tall. Skinny. Works out a lot. Short hair, like a GI cut."

"Color of the hair?"

"Dirty blond."

"How old would you figure?"

"Thirty-something."

"Here's my card, Raymundo. If you get any trouble, tickets or anything, please call me. Do you have a cellphone number?"

"Oh, no. That won't play, bro. No courtroom for me, no way. I give you something and that's it. Just wait and he'll come back."

"Who do you work for, Raymundo?"

"Man, I'm like you. The last of the independents. No paper on me. I see you around."

He took his bike and gracefully kick-glided it into traffic. I wished that I could do that.

The brownstones lined 65th Street down to the store at Madison Avenue. Their elegance and location made them cost upwards of five million. The millionaire owners had left for the beaches during this August heat wave. The precinct had a standing order for us cops to check for any burglary signs.

I tried doorknobs and checked the window glass.

One window had a sticker on it from the Goff Security Company. I phoned the number and asked them to call me at the Precinct if anyone had tried this doorknob and set off an alarm.

My feet felt gummy and dead in this heat.

ꟹ

A dark suit topped by a shaved head bobbed up out of the crowd. His squinty blue eyes hopscotched over me. He palmed a Deputy Inspector's gold shield. Sunlight lit the shield's blue enamel.

"Deputy Inspector Trask, Inspectional Services," the dark suit said.

I froze. Inspectional Services hunted us cops for any infraction.

"Yup," I said.

"By your name-tag, you're Royster. Are you supposed to be on Madison Avenue here, Officer? And what are your current Community Policing projects?"

Buses wheezed past us. Horns blew.

"I'm assigned to Third Avenue and 57th Street," I said. "And I've got no Community Policing projects because Community Policing does not work."

Trask stepped closer. He smelled of some manly-type after-shave.

"I'd like to hear your thinking on that," he said.

"Nossir."

"Speak, Officer. Or else we'll have trouble here."

"You won't listen."

"PO Royster, I'm giving you a reprimand for insubordination, being off-post and failing to meet standards."

"I meet my own standards," I said.

"And you will complete three ComPol projects, in writing, by this time next week."

My chin tucked down. It was a boxing habit.

"Sir, I'm new here," I said. "But in Brooklyn, us cops did real work. I'm not risking people's lives for some social experiment idea."

"I can have you fired for refusing this order," he said. "Loss of pension, medical, family dependents, *et cetera*, amounts to a one million dollar fine, over your lifetime. Be smart. Obey the order."

He scribbled in my memo book and left to fight crime somewhere.

Beat up, I leaned against a taxpayer's car.

☙

"Officer, can I ask you a question?" a short squatty woman with silver-gray hair drawled.

She sounded like a complication.

"Of course," I said by rote.

"Do you see that young man down the block looking into the cars?"

I had no idea who she was talking about.

"Where?" I asked.

She blew out a breath.

"Right there," she said. "In that red T-shirt."

Looking up, I glimpsed him. Deep in my thoughts, I had not noticed him before. But I did now. He was checking out each car that he passed, a good sixty feet from me. In his twenties, slight and agile, he looked like someone who would run.

I crossed the street to get closer.

He looked up, saw me and took off. His sneakers bobbed up and down. He hit the corner and vanished.

"Now he got away!" the citizen fumed.

To calm her, I put out his description over the radio. We could not arrest him for anything. The other cops would think that I had snapped my cap.

"Do I have to do your job for you?" she asked. "I park my car here every night."

"Thank you very much for your help," I said.

"Officer Royster," she said, reading my name-plate. "I may report you for incompetence."

Then I walked two rich blocks back to the 19th Precinct desk. The alarm company had called with an alarm just twenty minutes ago. I scribbled everything down in my memo book. A squinty-eyed Sergeant with a pug nose was busy spitting into a wastebasket.

"Sarge," I said. "I got a possible burglar scouting out spots today. He'll probably make his move tonight. Can you please get a car to cover this block tonight?"

He made me wait. You could hear him thinking.

I mentioned the alarm.

"You're the new boy?" he asked.

"Yup. Just in from a crummy dangerous precinct."

"How do you like the upper-class hoity-toity citizens here?" he asked.

"They don't think they need us."

"Yeah. That's why I'm retiring next year. All they do is bitch about us cops. And ask about ComPol. ComPol, what a joke."

"Now the burglar," I said.

"Everyone's off tonight," he said. "Summer time. And the boss isn't giving you humps any more chances to pad your overtime. He's hacked off at them for parking in his spot again."

"But it may go down tonight."

"It's not your townhouse, is it, Royster? You notified me. That's enough. Let them get burglarized. Remind them how things used to be."

"This is not sharp policing," I said.

I spun on my heel and tapped the planks out of the office.

ᴓ

Down the hall, a sign on the wall read "19th Precinct Anti-Crime. Sgt. Dunmoreland."

I knuckled the door and walked in.

A softening football player-type, with a gold sergeant's shield around his neck, looked me over.

"Sarge, I'm Royster. Can your anti-crime team help a cop out?" I asked.

His pouchy black face tightened under the dapper moustache. I told him what I had.

"Probably not tonight," he said. "We got a letter-writer on Park Avenue, screaming to the press how muggers are scaring him whenever he jogs. Calling us lazy. But we'll take a look sometime."

CHAPTER 2.

I stopped by the front desk.

Silva, a pretty-boy cop with glossy black hair long enough to enrage bosses, smirked above his undone reg necktie.

"How's the radio market?" I asked. "I'm going off-duty now."

He looked for bosses, saw none and slipped an NYPD radio from a drawer onto the desk. He swiveled so that he was looking away from me.

"It's needed, right, pal?"

"At my age, I can't toe-dance with some young cat-burglar type without an edge," I said. "This radio may keep from dying ahead of schedule."

"What I don't see, I don't see," he said. "The Job is looking to fire me anyway. Inspectional Services is snooping around today. So, what's a radio here or there? If a boss asks you about the radio, what do you say?"

"Go sandpaper a monkey," I said. "Silva, what is the word on our burglary deal here in the Playpen, the Upper East Side?"

"It's always a big deal with Captain Day, the summer."

Manhattan's Upper East Side houses some of the richest lords and their ladies in the world. When the weather turns sticky-hot, they just want us to protect their mansions and then head off to the Hampton beaches. Our mutts know this and crack into empty cribs while we waste time with ComPol projects."

Slipping the radio under my 3 XL Mickey Mouse T-shirt that covered my off-duty Glock, cuffs and ASP baton, I looked around the precinct house, expecting crowds of sergeants to descend on me.

"I'm ignoring ComPol today," I said. "I don't dislike the rich. Or obsess about them. I grew up entangled with them."

"Yeah?" Silva said.

"They are nothing new to me. I just hope that they ignore me while I po-lice their neighborhood the right way."

"But the bosses want ComPol," Silva said. "From 59th Street to 86th Street, burglars run wild. Why not? One brownstone can score them thousands in jewels, furs or electronics. Easy swag to unload. The only way to stop them is to catch them with meat in their mouth."

I made the steamy sidewalk without incident.

☙

Back on Madison Avenue, I bought a coffee, way light, and something hardish called a date roll to keep my engine running. Then I slouched on different brownstone stoops, looking for anyone who looked burglarish.

The fast-moving neighborhood rolled into rush hour. Impossible-looking fashion models walked borzois on leashes past me. They always wore boots even in this heat wave. Fashion counted more than comfort as they strode past, their boots tapping the sidewalk.

The usual fringe of people roved along East 65th Street. A sweaty jogger panted past, followed by more delivery types. That was sometimes the easiest way for a burglar to work, delivering take-out dinners and casing the places nearby.

Maybe back in the Middle Ages, dukes would ask peasants to bring them victuals and grog at night, knowing that the peasants might steal or murder them if they themselves went out.

But even lords and ladies needed their food.

Some things did not change.

Millionaires could not live without their sushi.

The heat tightened after sundown. Nothing cooled. My blue jeans stuck to me, tighter than the bag.

Moving took an effort.

No cop cars, no RMPs, Radio Motor Patrol cars, rolled past.

"As usual," I muttered. "It feels like our hero is holding the line alone for civilization against the barbarian hordes."

My flanks stiffened.

"The good bosses of the 19th Precinct would be unhappy with me working off-duty," I said to myself. "They think that initiative is for salesmen. All kinds of ugly civil liability issues will arise. The city will never back me. If I see a bad rascal, 911 is the number to play."

☙

Hours dragged by.

Night came.

I moved a bit.

Nobody noticed me. Nobody called to have cops brace me for sitting on a stoop. The brownstoners had indeed left the block.

This was ripe pickings.

My head slipped back.

Dozing felt good and natural.

Midnight came and went.

"In six hours, I'm getting back up to do real police work," I yawned. "The cops who think that I'm crazy, a Funny Bunny, may be right."

Sleep felt sweet.

Tired enough, you can sleep anywhere.

☙

Glass shattered a block away.

I rose up off the stoop, feet dragging.

Nobody else was on the street.

Hugging the building line, I tried running towards the sound and crossed Madison Avenue.

Dead quiet answered me back.

The block held more brownstones and a couple of shops, closed up tight. I stayed back, feeling like a kid playing pirates.

A woman screamed, close by.

"East Six-six between Madison and Park," I said into the radio. "Off-duty MOS requests 10-85, possible 10-31 in progress."

A squeal sounded inside the radio.

"Another dead zone for radios," I muttered to myself.

I jogged down the block, trying to get a signal so I could broadcast out.

The woman screamed again, behind me now.

"10-39, possible attack in progress!" I shouted into the radio.

"10-5!" a voice shouted back over the radio. "Repeat your location! You're coming in broken!"

"East Six-six and Madison!" I shouted.

The woman screamed, long and terrifying.

The brownstone from where she was screaming loomed over me. No lights showed inside. Two trim balconies jutted out from the second floor. The burglar must have gotten in that way.

I tried the front door. Locked. I stepped back and flung myself at the door. The door held. My shoulder cracked.

"Sprain! Let that be a sprain!" I panted.

I kicked out near the doorknob. Sometimes you could pop the lock.

The door sagged in an inch. But it stayed shut.

I leaped back outside, jumped onto the wrought-iron fence, balanced and lunged upwards.

My hands hit the fence. They slipped off.

"This leaping around is for someone else," I said.

I jumped up again and grabbed on.

The woman screamed again.

I got a sneaker against the wall and forced myself up.

Across the street, windows went up.

"Call the police!" I shouted, gasping. "Right now!"

I got up onto the three-foot balcony. The window was down. I tried opening it.

Locked.

I tucked my head down, hands into wet armpits and crashed through the window.

It shattered all over me. Something pricked the back of my neck.

Music floated somewhere inside the brownstone. I knew the music.

She screamed again.

Everything was dark.

I was in a living room. Furniture barked my shins.

My hands went to a wall, looking for a light switch. It helped if you lived here.

She was screaming upstairs.

I got to a staircase and ran upwards.

I wanted to trap him high, running towards the roof.

I got onto the landing.

The music got louder.

Half-light lit a bedroom.

She twisted naked on the bed. Her skin showed silver.

A tall shape held her down. His back was to me.

I yanked out the ASP, a folding metal baton, unsnapped it and slammed it for his legs.

Three feet of steel THWOCKED! into his legs.

He buckled and went down.

I swung again, aiming for his head.

The ASP caught something else first. The something else broke. Maybe it was a Ming vase.

I swung again.

An arm gripped my legs.

I jumped back.

The wall blocked me.

Something slammed my face BAM!

Bones crinkled in my neck.

I tasted blood.

He hit me again. My radio dropped.

The floor slammed my ear.

I swung the ASP.

"You hit me!" the woman screamed. "Don't hit ME!"

More things broke.

He was somewhere behind me in the dark.

I kept my free hand out to touch him. This was no time to draw my gun. He was tougher, younger and stronger than me.

Everyone was. He could take the gun from me and use it.

Or else I might shoot and hit the woman.

Feet pounded the stairs, going down.

Keeping the ASP in front of me as a feeler, I rose up and moved to the stairs.

His feet sounded ahead of me.

He was running to the back of the house.

Glass broke.

He crashed through something.

I ran towards the noise.

A wide picture window was shattered.

Light from other houses showed a wide backyard.

People shouted.

"Police officer!" I shouted.

I could see him twenty feet ahead of me. It was my first look at him.

He was rangy and topped six feet, moving fast. He wore a dark windbreaker, glossy letters on it.

The letters read "POLICE."

"Hold it!" someone bellowed to my left.

It sounded like a cop. I dropped.

BAM! BAM!

Shots fired.

I could not hear anything.

My ears burned.

"I'm a cop!" I croaked. "Idiot! You're shooting at nothing."

My voice broke.

"Don't shoot!" I said louder.

"Holster that! Are you nuts?" another voice said.

The suspect in the POLICE windbreaker whipped around and faced me. Shadows hid his face.

"Watch the mutt!" the suspect in the windbreaker said. "I'm a cop!"

He waved the radio. I recognized it as my radio.

"No, he's not!" I shouted. "I'm the cop!"

"Nobody do nothing!" another voice shouted. "This is a grand mess!"

The suspect in the POLICE windbreaker stepped towards me, stared and then vaulted up to a fence between brownstones.

He pulled himself over and was gone in the darkness.

"PO Royster!" I shouted. "Off-duty! The perp's getting away."

"Don't move, champ," the second voice ordered. "Or else I put a big hole in you."

The suspect was gone.

I could see nothing in the darkness.

Sucking in my breath, I ran for the same fence. My arms stretched out. I slammed into it. My chin ached. It spat blood.

"I'll shoot!" the second voice said.

"Hope not," I whispered.

Somehow, I got over the fence. The suspect was running thirty feet ahead of me. I slopped after him. He threw the POLICE jacket away.

"Shoot him!" the first voice shouted

"We can't! You know that. No weapon showing," a new voice said.

The suspect ran onto Madison Avenue.

A crowd of party-types weaved back and forth on the sidewalk. They blocked his path.

I lunged.

My fingers caught his belt. I yanked him down onto the sidewalk and fell on top of him. The crowd whooped and parted. They looked like office workers, going for dinner and beers in the heat wave.

"Police! Freeze!"

"Help me!" the suspect shouted. "This cop's crazy! He just beat me up! He'll kill me!"

"Let him go!" a husky kid shouted. "He didn't do anything!"

"Cops are bullies, man!" another one said. "Hitting on us!"

"No cops!"

Someone kicked my elbow. My arm went dead. The suspect glared at me. Very pale skin mixed with glacier-blue eyes. His blond GI haircut shone.

"Please! Help me!" he shouted.

A woman hit my neck. Her boyfriend reached down and slugged me. My head sang.

"Back off or I'll hurt you!" I shouted.

"You can't!"

Another fist walloped me. Pricey shoes scraped my ribs.

The suspect rolled to his feet, ran across Madison and was gone.

I reached for my ribs.

"He's gonna shoot us!"

They skittered uptown, heels clacking.

I sank down, paralyzed and heaving up bile.

"Stomped by the upper class," I said. "Good accents and better teeth. Rich clothes. Think that one over."

CHAPTER 3.

I limped back to the brownstone, bent over.

The front door was open now.

Cops always create chaos.

"You're working off-duty, pal?" A young cop wearing blue jean shorts and shield on a neck-chain stared at me. "You must be nuts."

"That's Royster," another anti-crime cop with a scruffy beard said. "We got a phone call on him. He's a cuckoo bird. A Funny Bunny."

"Shield's in my back left pocket," I said. "Off-duty piece, right hip."

"Where'd you get the radio, pal? You off-duty?"

"Not when I hear a scream," I said.

"He made it worse!" the woman screeched behind me. I whipped around. She yanked the cord of her bathrobe tightly. Savage hair tumbled over an exquisite face now twisted by anger. Her slim jaws clenched, showing her perfect teeth.

"I had him calmed down," she said. "He was going to leave with some jewelry. Then this fool broke through my window and got him all stirred up. Then he fondled me and threatened to kill me. All because of you!"

"Did you invite him in?" the cop in shorts asked. "Maybe you should marry him."

"Probably eligible," another voice said.

"Definitely straight," the bearded one said.

"You screamed," I said. "And then I moved. You were screaming forever before I crashed your window."

"You guys shut up!" Sarge Dunmoreland from Anti-Crime said. "That you, Royster? Why did you shoot?"

That stopped me.

"I didn't shoot!" I said. "It stayed in the holster!"

"Okay, okay," Sarge said. "Who fired?"

Nobody moved.

"Come on, come on." The Sarge said.

"Oh, I did," the cop on my left said.

He looked slight and ratty, somebody's afterthought, with an underbite and a bald spot covered by greasy long hair.

"Yeah, that was me, Sarge."

"You just dummied up when I asked. What's the matter? Stage fright?"

"I was just formulating my answer." he said.

"That what you call it?"

"I fired because I saw a gun." he said, gulping.

"Who had the gun? This nut Royster?"

"I don't know. Maybe."

"Thanks," I said.

"No, I think it was the other guy," he said. "Pretty sure."

"Get more sure," the Sarge said. "Because the Duty Captain's rolling on this, this –"

"Hairball," I said.

"Royster, shut up. They should psycho you out."

"Our captain's going to scream about this," one cop said.

"Captain Day just lost his son. He's coming apart more each day."

"Tonight won't glue him back together, that's for sure."

"Sarge, the Playpen fools blocked me," I said. "Some comfy upper-class junior execs. For kicks. Get me back to the Brooklyn slums where things are normal."

"They hate us in this precinct," the Sarge said. "I never knew why."

"Me, neither," another cop said.

"Maybe there is no reason."

"There's a lot of that going around."

"The perp had a radio!" another cop said.

"Royster, you know anything about the radio? Maybe you two were working together?"

"What?" I asked. "No way. That was my radio. I dropped it. He grabbed it."

"They fire cops for losing radios."

"They fire cops for giving bosses bad dreams," I said. "This was no burglar, Sarge. This is a sex deviate. What they call 'a Horn Bug.'"

CHAPTER 4.

"Please come inside, PO Royster," Captain Day said. "Would you care to sit or to stand?"

My gullet went up and down in my throat. I dropped my chin to cover it.

"I'll sit, sir," I said.

"Me, too," Day smiled. "Too much of policing gets done on our feet, holding a slice of pizza in one hand and a cell-phone in another."

Day showed a grandfatherly pinkish face under a shock of wooly white hair. Gold eyeglasses shielded blue eyes. A paunch softened the body in the uniform white shirt. A strong whiff of cologne came from his perfectly pressed dark blue uniform.

"Let's see if we can clarify what happened last night, shall we?" Day said.

"It seems that you got a tip on a burglar, could not get anyone to move on it and staked it out yourself. A melee took place. A shot was fired, the mope got away and a very persuasive victim who used to be an actress has been giving me hell from this phone all morning. Right?"

Talking seemed called for.

If I dummied up, he could order me to talk.

"Now, I appreciate you speaking to me without dragging in your PBA union rep," Day said. "You had an interesting time in your last precinct in Brooklyn. The book lists you with three felony arrests, eleven misdemeanor arrests and twenty-three summonses in the last month. Plus, you recruited two applicants for the Academy. Recruiting is tough when they only pay twenty-five K to start. You're a hard worker, it seems. So let's see if we can look at this mess together."

"That's fine with me. I sketched the perp from memory. And I gave a copy to the squad. They may send it down to the Sketch Unit at Police Plaza."

I showed him my original sketch. The Horn Bug had a narrow head, ears set close and a sharp chin. If people were dogs, he would be a slim Doberman pinscher.

"Good, good. I admire your work ethic in doing this on your own time. Now, I'm sure that you believe in Community Policing."

"No."

He frowned. I had ruined the moment. Again.

Day's eyes burned, then calmed. Something bad inside was hurting him.

Maybe he was pondering his dead son.

"Royster, how would you define 'Community Policing'?" he asked.

"A farce, Captain."

"I don't disagree with you, Royster. But the Mayor, the Commissioner and the think-tank virgins who run this city push it."

"Let them push."

"It's an idea that is hot right now. When I came on the job, they screamed 'No corruption!' 'Don't trust Patrol!' Fashions change."

"Meanwhile, crime rips the poor," I said.

"I'm sure that you have a number of ComPol contacts and projects that you have written down."

"No, I haven't. The people on my beat talk with me. When I call them my 'beatniks,' they smile."

"Touching, Royster."

"I don't try fooling my beatniks with fake ComPol projects."

"Nobody is old enough to remember the first real beatniks." Day said. "They believed in beatnik poetry, bongo drums and looking weird in the 1950's. You're just confusing people by calling them beatniks."

"Some remember, Captain. And they like the attention I give them,"

"Royster, I can help you out of this mess," Day said. "I'll do it because you're a worker. And I need workers to make me look good so I can make Deputy Inspector before I retire next year."

I swallowed.

"I'm 46 and need the health benefits," I said. "What should I do?"

"Write up that today you had cultivated some ComPol friends on your beat. You helped them with non-police problems. In return, one of them tipped you to this burglar, this sex bandit."

"But that didn't happen."

"Let me finish. You relied on your new ComPol friend. But he screwed up the address where the burglar was going to hit. When it happened, you had to respond rapidly. That's how this mess with the other cops went down. Okay?"

"Do I name names?"

"Yup. But nobody will ever check, believe me. I'll use my juice downtown with Internal Affairs and that new CRIT Unit to quash the investigation."

"CRIT?" I asked. "That's a new cop acronym?"

"Critical Response Incident Team," Day said. "Dress it up as a ComPol attempt that bounced wrong. And your career will survive."

My feet flexed again. Running out of this office looked attractive right now.

"Captain, let me see if I understand," I said. "You want me to write up a false statement that I have to swear to?"

"If you don't, the Job may fire you."

"But writing that statement can get me fired just as well."

"Nobody will check. Believe me."

He shook his head. The cologne smell came back again. But it was not cologne. I was sure now. It was a whiskey smell. Captain Day had been taking on giggle water, safe in his office.

Maybe he had just lost a tooth.

"Captain, I appreciate you helping me. But I'll go with what really happened."

He bugged out his blue eyes.

"Royster, nobody normal will believe your story from last night. You told your sergeant that middle-class white kids blocked you from grabbing that perp."

"They did, Cap. I'm still new at dealing with the wealthy in Manhattan," I said.

"That's obvious."

"Before today, I only policed slums. In slums, they may hate cops. But they know they need us. It's different here."

"How so?"

"These bluebloods in your 19th Precinct don't seem to care about crime. Those fools that blocked me last night had good accents, good teeth and expensive clothes. Why did they stop me from catching that Horn Bug? What's going on in this precinct?"

"Apathy, perhaps. Crime is down."

"But ComPol won't help it. Neither will a false report."

His face closed up like the dials of a safe. The bones and fat meshed together and color flooded into his cheeks.

Liquor was reddening up the granddad's eyes behind the gold glasses.

"Captain, I always treat my beatniks right," I said. "And they respect me because I don't pretend to be Mister Fix-it, the Shell Answer Man or Jesus Christ with a Glock nine. No fancy terms. I'm their beat cop."

"You seem fixated on fighting good advice," Day said.

His voice got growly. He was losing whatever cool he had bragged to himself about before.

"Your previous commanders noted it on your record. Seems that you have turned down inside jobs and special details just to stay out on the street. At your age of 46, that seems odd."

"Captain, what happens if I catch this burglar, this Horn Bug?" I asked.

He made a face.

"Royster, good luck with that. You're not sharp enough."

"But if I do?"

"You know that public opinion drives the Job," he said. "Catch him and you're a hero. Nobody can touch you then. But you're not sharp enough to catch him. You can't do it."

Day leaned forward. My feet twitched, to run away from him.

"Do you have many fantasies like this?" he asked. "It's abnormal. Are you normal, Royster?"

"As normal as the day is long, Cap."

"Well, PO Royster, days get pretty short in the winter."

"Here are some letters," I said, taking out an envelope from my locker. "Not just commendations, either. They're from people in my Brooklyn command. They prove what I just said, about handling crime by working and not fancy ComPol theories."

Day took the letters and scanned them.

His office grew quiet. Awards decorated his walls, with the blue-and-gold-enamel design cherished by the NYPD.

Photos of a slimmer Day, with dark hair and thinner glasses and no belly, showed how time hit all of us.

"One of these letters is from Al Lipkin, Manhattan North Homicide," Day said. "He says that you're valuable to the Department. Why would he say that?"

"Because I am."

"I know the names of some of these bosses, Royster. They've retired."

"That means that they can speak the truth."

"Meaning that I cannot?"

"Meaning that you are still concerned with your next promotion."

"Captain is the last rank in this Department to test for," Day said. "Above that, the brass has to like me. They won't like me if I let the 335 cops in this command ignore ComPol. So, I have to land on you. Harshly."

He sucked in a breath and tore the letters in half.

My head jerked back like someone was jabbing at me.

I sucked in a deep one and thought about the Valley of the Kings in Egypt. Or any other place. Just not this tiny Dickensian room.

"I've got copies," I blurted out.

"I don't care."

"Some of those were official Department memos."

"I don't care about that, either."

He smiled like a tyrant about to bastinado some rebel's sweet and tender spots with a skewer.

"Captain, technically, you're asking me to break the law by that false report."

He smiled.

"What false report?" he asked.

The office sank into more quiet.

I sucked in a deep breath.

"Captain, at this time, I'm formally requesting a PBA delegate sit in with us."

His face flamed more.

"Are you nuts?" he asked. "That's what your bosses have always wondered."

"That's always a hard question to answer."

"Well, I think that you're deranged. You can't sit down with me, dislike what is said and then bail out with your union rep. Nossir."

I stood up.

The whiskey smell came back.

"Then our talk is over, sir," I said.

"That's insubordination!"

He lurched up and threw a sloppy right hand punch. It brushed my jaw. My teeth bit my tongue. I fell backwards. A chair slammed to the floor.

Day grappled with me. The whiskey smell covered me.

Someone wrenched the door open behind me. Hands gripped me. I went into the wall. My shoulder screamed with pain. A chair hit my ankle. Cops filled the room.

"Royster is a psycho!" Day said. "He assaulted me. You're suspended. Surrender your shield and weapon."

Sgt. Kipides, the Integrity Control Officer, a paunchy pushover and a bootlicker, slipped out his handcuffs. I dodged.

"Easy, Sarge," I said. "The captain assaulted me. Smell his breath. That's booze."

Kipides helped Day sit back down. So did the other three cops.

"I don't smell anything," Kipides said.

"Me, neither," another said.

"Hey, I smell something," one cop said.

"No, you don't," Kipides said. "Better not. Cap's going through some trouble, that's all."

I unclipped the suede off-duty holster with the Glock Nine inside and the worn black leather shield case. The thick silver biscuit of the shield glowed. I dropped both on the desk.

"Royster, I'm calling for an ambulance to lock you down in Bellevue Hospital forthwith," Day said.

I froze.

"That's not legal," I said. My voice shook again. "Not without two doctor's signatures."

"Kipides, call two cars and a bus for here," Day said, using the word "bus" as cop-speak for "ambulance."

"Cap, he's right on that," Kipides said.

"And there's no indie witness that I'm violent," I said. "Get me a PBA rep here now."

"No PBA rep," Day said. "Too many fools in here now."

"The Patrol Guide gives me ten days before I have to go inside a hospital," I said. My voice cracked.

"No, it doesn't," Day said.

He was back in his chair now and in command.

"Boss, I'm afraid that Royster's correct," Kipides said. "On an involuntary commitment, he does have ten days. You don't want him slipping out on a technicality."

"Put him in anyway," Day said.

The others shifted.

"We can't," Kipides said. "Let him walk today. What can he do in ten days?"

Day looked up at everyone. I could see the fear in his eyes. He worried about losing respect, his precinct and his strength.

A wrong move could make him an old man.

"When you come back in ten days," Day said, "I'm going to bury you in Bellevue, Royster. They will never let you out, after what I write up. And mental patients don't get a trial. They just get hearings. And I can sway those hearings."

"I'm gonna stop the Horn Bug," I said. "Try swaying that."

"Get out," Day said. "Enjoy your ten days."

CHAPTER 5.

When Day took my gun and shield, I floated out of his office, my ankles flashing down the wooden staircase.

I might fly off the edge of the earth.

Other cops' faces, beefy, unshaven and hurting, flashed past above the dark blue uniform shirts. Their creaking gun-belts seemed to mock me.

"Hey, Maxy?" one cop asked.

His cowlick poked up against a fleshy subway face, crumpled by use like a cardboard coffee cup.

"I got to cut out," I said. "Before someone asks to see my shield. That's the price of the ticket to this boy's club here."

He stared at me.

An idea hit me.

I stopped at my locker and loaded up a duffle bag I kept there for emergencies.

☙

The pavement bounced back waves of heat at me.

A block before I reached them, crowds of lithe Hunter college kids parted to let me cut through them.

I sank down on the stone bench molded against the wall.

Bright chirpy kids eddied around.

"Gotta get on the good foot," I muttered.

Day would lock me down into an asylum in ten days. Those eyes showed that he meant to do it.

If I were not crazy now, living behind bars in a psych ward would do the trick.

"Get on the good foot," I told myself. "Get up."

I tried rising.

Nothing worked.

My body was screwed to on the stone bench.

"This is impossible."

I tried getting up on that good foot.

Passersby stared at me.

My body rocked on the stone.

My hands shook worse than before.

"Catatonic-type stuff," I whispered. "Shock corridor. If I stay stuck to that bench," I whispered, "Day will come scrape me off and trundle me to Bellevue Hospital like a trussed-up Bengal tiger with a toothache. I can never stop moving now."

At last, I was standing and covering concrete, heading uptown.

As I walked, I phoned different lawyers and a few friends. The phone simmered in my sweaty hand. Nobody was available for a chat. Everyone's voicemail said that they would call me back.

I needed help and all the professionals were now tied up.

The Upper East Side, the Playpen, swirled around me.

Bright designer colors and frivolous party stores ignored my troubles. This whirl-a-gig social scene would spin around while I rotted in my hospital room, a forty-minute walk away.

My feet kept moving.

The streets started to change.

The stores got narrower. Fewer trashcans held down the corners. Salsa music played somewhere.

I was crossing the boundary into the Barrio of Spanish Harlem.

Finally, I reached my PBA lawyer, Simon, and told him today's misery.

"I've never had anything like this in front of me," he said. "I'll have my paralegal research this."

"That's a relief."

"The Captain actually promised to stop the action if you caught this pervert? That's nutty on his part."

"Glad we agree. I've got a wild idea to catch him."

"It sounds like you better not tell me this wild idea," he said.

"Okay."

"I'll try to help. But first you have to show good faith by going inside Bellevue."

I stopped dead on the sidewalk.

"What?"

"There is no better way to convince the court that you are sane," he said.

"Then why don't YOU go into a padded cell?"

"Just go. Treat it like a vacation. Meanwhile, me and my paralegal will be working to get you out."

I shut my eyes. Others bumped into me and ricocheted back into their self-absorbed lives.

"And what about your days off, national holidays when court is closed, coffee breaks, lunches?" I said. "Meanwhile, I'm inside, listening to my roommates handle confinement in charming ways. What if you get hit by a falling septic tank and some other lawyer has to take over your case? That's my body rotting in there."

"They have a gym."

"Then you use it. Two months inside, and I will go crazy for real."

I snapped the phone shut.

Nerves made me cough.

My head whipped from side to side.

☙

On the frontier streets between the Playpen and the Barrio, I entered a huge store that sold everything from toys to *quincienera* dresses to electronics parts.

My wild idea took hold again and quickened my breathing.

I bought a few items and stuffed them in my duffle bag.

Then I entered a storefront marked "Taino Health Club" a few doors off Lexington Avenue at 105th Street.

Inside, beat-up leather boxing bags hung from the ceiling. Two high-schoolers in headgear sparred in a corner. A smell of old leather hung in the air. Cracks ran through the walls.

The woman who unfolded from a chair stood a foot less than my six feet. Honey-colored hair hung next to blue-tinted glasses over a catlike mobile face. Strength showed in her tense forearms and wrists.

"Why, Mister Royster," she purred in a prairie-state Kansas drawl. "You do take a girl's breath away, arriving unannounced."

It took something to answer. So I chattered a bit.

Above us, someone played a sad mambo song.

"I'm in trouble, Nancy," I said. "And I need a favor."

"Pray tell, Mister Royster."

"Real fighting. All you can teach me."

"We teach boxing here."

"I need what you don't teach the others."

"Do you want to sign up for boxing lessons? We have a special going."

"That time I found your lover with the cocaine and helped him get rehab instead of the joint? Remember?"

"My fancy-man Santiago," she sighed. "He's still my heartthrob, I do declare."

"It's time to pay back that favor," I said. "Today."

"Why?"

"Because I'm going someplace without a gun or a stick. They might tear me apart. So I need your fighting stuff."

"How come you never asked before, Officer?"

"The Academy taught us enough, following the law. Where I'm going, there's no law."

"My sweet, I can't teach you stuff that will get me arrested or sued," she said. "Some of these moves can kill."

"Nobody will ever know who taught me," I said. "I'll blame the Dim Mak wizards on the back pages of Marvel comics."

"That's what you say today."

"Santiago, your fancy-man, was headed upstate for a telephone number," I said.

"What's a telephone number?"

"Numbers put together. Like three-three-five. That many years to run out his sentence. I risked my job, jail and pension myself to show you some compassion. Now I want a consideration for what I did."

She stayed quiet.

"Come in back," she said at last.

ꕤ

We went into another room with mats on the floor and heavy bags hung on chains.

She leaned against me, smelling of vanilla and patchouli.

"Do we really want to learn hitting today?" she asked.

"That's all I want."

"How come you stay aloof from me, Officer Royster? Most men don't."

"I'll bet they don't."

"So you're becoming a challenge for me. I can't melt you?"

"Some other time. Some other place. Some other man."

"Boxing is the world's best system for how to hold your hands," she said. "They guard the chin and throat. Elbows cover ribs. Hands can guard or strike. But everyone's hands can break. You're hitting someone with a frail bag of 215 bones."

I made a fist and tapped it against the cracked wall. The frail bag of bones hurt.

"So we forget punches to the head," she went on. "Open those fists. Hit with the palm. You get more power that way. Punch the bag with a fist."

I jabbed. The bag stirred three or four inches.

"Now the palm, fingers tucked out of the way."

I struck. The bag danced back seven inches.

"In boxing, you lose power at the wrist. With the palm heel, physics of the hand makes it stronger. And you cannot break your palm. Hit a tree trunk or a brick wall, if you wish."

I tapped the wall with my palm. It smacked but it did not hurt me. With more power, I tried it again.

"You're right," I said.

"Turn that palm heel to one side. Keep the knuckles flexed back. Thumb in so he cannot grab it for a lock. Now chop with the side of that hand. Jaw, temple, neck, eyes, nose. Again, you cannot hurt your hand this way."

She showed me how to hit the bag.

"Another last-ditch move," she said. "When you're losing and on the ground, roll onto your stomach. Give him your back. He'll come in to strangle you. Push up with your palms and kick back with one or two feet. It's called 'the mule kick.' Keep doing it or he'll kill you."

"Why don't they teach this stuff?" I asked, feeling stupid. Again.

"Some do. Rape prevention classes teach it. So do some self-defense courses. But trainers don't make money teaching it. You learn it in two minutes and practice it at home. Or against a tree."

Nancy knitted her brows prettily.

"We trainers need to survive while paying Manhattan rents," she said. "That means teaching students long-term. It can take years to learn boxing, karate or the mixed-martial-arts style of jujitsu."

"And the cash rolls in," I said.

"Trickles in. Don't forget we also get customers into good physical shape, make them feel better and less afraid. That saves them from getting hurt. "

She taught me low kicks, how to blade my body to protect the soft stuff, elbow strikes and other tricks.

"This mess is exhausting," I said.

"Dull, too. No fancy Asian names. That's why youngsters ignore it."

"So why do thousands of people study martial arts?"

"Martial arts, karate and all that, works sometimes," she replied. "But, for most, it is a kind of therapy. They want to get into shape, have a place to go and be a part of something. You don't look convinced. Okay. Come at me."

I stepped in.

She kicked my shin. That stopped me.

Her palm tapped my chin and throat. Fingertips touched my eyes.

Her other foot touched my instep.

"Don't move, Max."

An elbow was at my temple.

Her honey-colored hair came over the smoky left eye.

"I can do this all over again," she breathed. "It takes almost nothing to learn. And you don't need to be strong to use it. Smashing your instep ends the attack. Now, we try the classic karate response. Come at me again and, this time, resist."

I obeyed.

She threw a high karate kick. I brushed it aside. Another kick came at me. I dodged it and slapped her foot down. She threw two punches at my belly. I let them land.

They rocked me back. But I kept moving on her.

"See?" she said. "Karate did not stop you. Even a groin kick won't slow a street fighter who wants to hurt me. As a pro, I would use the dirty fighting tricks that I'm teaching you today."

"Now I'll try a jujitsu lock," she said.

She gripped my forearm.

I slithered out of it.

Her fingers gripped my elbow.

I went to the mat and rolled free.

"You need to practice locks all the time for them to work," she said.

"I don't have that much free time," I said. "Yet."

"Nobody normal does."

"I feel silly," I said. "After all my knocking around, I did not know how well this stuff works."

"That's because you can't practice it without hurting someone. Sooner or later, you'll nail them."

"Lawsuits terrify the Academy. So they teach us mostly defensive moves that do not work."

"Now a jujitsu takedown," she said.

She circled in, gripped my waist and threw me to the mat.

I kept rolling and came up with my hands cocked to strike.

She came in and put hands on me again.

"While I'm doing this, how many times can you jab me?" she asked.

"About six."

"One jab can knock me out. See the problem?"

"And they sell it to make money?"

"Jujitsu/Mixed Martial Arts is America's fastest growing sport. With 27 rules like, 'Do not touch the throat, eyes or ears'. So it is still a game."

"No rules in my world."

"Just like the street." Her eyes glowed. "Tell me about it, Max."

"You wouldn't believe me."

"That sounds hot."

"Steaming."

"Practice these moves every night."

"I hate to exercise."

"Every night." She checked the outer gym. "Those two boxer-types have left, Max. I'll lock the door and we can be alone."

She leaned in against me. Her spring-steel body arched against mine. I tried dodging with the steps just learned.

"Let me go out, and then you can lock the door," I rasped. "Be alone with yourself."

"Why so flip? Don't you trust me, Max?"

"Sure."

"Then why not?"

"Something tells me to keep moving. I can't afford tenderness. I have to be a blunt instrument that never looks back."

CHAPTER 6.

When I left the studio, it felt like a black inky cloud was covering me.

"Three years ago, our hero would drown this with whiskey," I muttered. "But now, we're going to walk."

I strode down Lexington Avenue, following the car and bus traffic under an oily gray sky.

I called the 19th Precinct detectives.

"Why don't you grow up, Royster?" Detective Wang said in a wheezy smoker's voice. "Just ride out your suspension. We're real busy, but if you got a sketch of this mutt, fax it to us. We'll try looking, like you say."

Manhattan Sex Crimes said the same thing.

Using my own cash, I faxed them my rough pencil sketch from a café.

"They're just telling me the story of Goliath and the lion," I said. "Their bosses will not let them hunt around just on my tip. Not in this department."

Then I stepped into the Franklin Hotel Garage on East 87th Street, just off Lexington.

"Max," Leo said in his thick Puerto Rican accent. He stood at the garage ramp. Before I turned cop, I had known Leo for years in the neighborhood. He was one of my beatniks who helped me whenever he could.

He looked as dark and stumpy as the cheroots that he smoked. An accident had chopped off three fingers on his right hand and two on the left. But he kept smiling, drinking vodka and laughing through everything.

I stepped down into the bathroom, opened the duffle bag and took out my first-class summer police uniform. I put it on, along with the Sam Browne gunbelt.

The toy police kit from the store included a black plastic Glock with a red-tipped barrel. I fitted it into my regulation holster and could not tell the difference from the real thing.

The toy gray plastic shield was the trickiest part. The size was right but the words "City Police" marked it as a toy. I bent the plastic back between my thumbs so that nobody could read the words "City Police."

Then I lit a match and held the flame close to the shield. The word "City" blurred from the flame. The word "Police" stayed firm. The number "1065" showed in the lower panel, just like my real police shield.

In my black leather holder with its decoration ribbons, the shield might pass in dim light.

No New Yorker could tell you what words are on the real police shield. Nobody but cops bothered to look or remember. And nobody expected to see a fake cop or a suspended one like me, patrolling as a fake.

I fitted on the hat with the cap device. The numbers were my real shield number, 11964. But nobody would notice that. If they did, I would spin them a tale about switched hats.

My palms wetted as I stepped out of the bathroom in uniform. This might not work.

"You working undercover?" Leo asked.

"You have no idea. Hold onto my duffle bag. I'll be back in a couple of hours."

I heaved a sickening sharp breath and stepped out onto nighttime Manhattan as a real fake cop.

ᴙ

Nobody gave me a second look when I came up the ramp and walked west to Central Park.

There, the darkness would cover me.

The toy radio rode inside my radio carrier on the gunbelt.

I thumbed my cellphone alive, switched to Wonder Radio USA and got the NYPD police band.

"Seven-David, Seven-David," the radio broadcast the dispatcher's voice. "Possible 10-54 on Delancey and Essex."

"Seven-David, 10-4. 'kay," came the voice of the responding cop.

I put the cellphone in my hip pocket, near the radio, making it sound as if the toy radio itself were broadcasting.

But nobody would notice.

A blonde woman with rhinestone and sea-green eyeglasses jogged past, tugged along by a black Labrador dog on leash.

To break my stage fright, I smiled at her and nodded.

"Evening, ma'am." I said, fighting to sound normal.

She just kept running.

So much for ComPol.

My uniform Reeboks ferried me down as far as 65th Street close to Fifth Avenue. Sketch in hand, I started canvassing the street.

"Excuse me, sir," I said to the first man I encountered, who was clicking open the door to his BMW.

He was a polo-shirt-and-chino-pants blue-blood, in his virile fifties, with an aquiline profile.

"I can't talk," the man said. "I'm very busy right now."

"I'm checking on something bad that happened here on Monday," I went on.

"I said, 'I'm busy'. Is this something important?"

His tone made me step back.

"Attempted rape and burglary," I said. "On your block."

"Come, come. I did not hear a word about this." He said. "This block is very secure."

"Sir, it happened."

"If you say so. But that's your concern. Not mine."

He shook his head, piled into his BMW and drove off.

"Where is care?" I asked aloud.

☙

I reached Park Avenue without joy.

A man was speed-walking uptown. Cottony white hair topped a sharp outdoor face. He wore the lightweight dark blue suit, hand-painted tie and glossy black shoes of the world-shaker power broker. All the pretty people with the tucked-in tummies were out tonight. To look that perfect took a lot of money.

Feeling like a vacuum cleaner salesperson, I sucked in a breath.

"Excuse me, sir," I said. "Police Officer Max Royster, 19th Precinct. Do you have a minute?"

He scanned my sketch.

"I've seen him over on East 83rd Street," he said.

That stopped me.

"You have?" I asked.

"Absolutely."

"What was he doing?"

"You'll excuse me, officer. But I'm running way late for a meeting."

"This is important."

"So is my meeting. I've got your name. I'll contact you at the station house."

I took three quick steps just to keep up with him.

"What is your phone number, sir?" I asked.

"Officer Royster, I have to leave."

No law gave me the juice to hold him. If I angered him now, he might never call me again.

So I watched him speed away.

His shoes pumped the pavement.

"Everyone here is in big rush," I said. "Billing the client or something."

But I had the 83rd Street connection. And Mr. Speed-walker seemed very sure of it, along with everything else.

☙

I did this canvass a few more times, moving east on the streets.

I called the One-Nine again and gave my name.

"Yeah, Royster," Detective Keller said. "We heard all about your big night here. Are you okay?"

I gave him the tip about East 83rd Street.

"That's not much help," he said. "But I'll pass it along. Nobody normal is going to do much about it."

"There's that word 'normal' again."

I went back to my canvass.

Then raindrops hit my fingers holding the sketch. I ignored them. The person that I was bothering did the same.

But the rain got stronger and then, it hit.

Playpenners scurried into doorways or tucked copies of *The Times* over their heads.

"No street corner canvassing now," I said.

All the stores were closed.

There was nobody to talk to here.

☙

Feeling bolder now, I walked up to Leo's garage. I shucked off the damp uniform and hung it in his spare locker. The gunbelt, fake shield and radio stayed with it.

"Nobody got the key but me," Leo said. "Don't worry nothing."

He saw me change back into my street clothes, shook hands and watched me leave.

Pictures of me wearing mental hospital greens and sleeping on a hard ward bed went through my mind.

I phoned Simon, my PBA lawyer, again. He was gone already. His voicemail message grated in my ear.

Then I called the Subway Inn at 60th and Lexington, the cop bar for the 19th Precinct.

"Yeah, Subway Inn," Cal the bartender said.

"Internal Affairs CRIT has a sting going on, East 83rd Street," I whispered. "Tell the other cops to watch it."

"Where?"

I killed the call.

"That will start the rumors a-flying," I said to myself. "Cops will stay away. Human nature always wins out."

The bored CUNY guard nodded as I entered Hunter College and made my way to the Rathskeller Lounge on the second floor.

"Tonight is open mike night for stand-up comedy," I thought. "Let's see if ComPol can work some tricks for our hero tonight."

Nursing a black coffee to wire myself up, I sat at the bar and scanned the others. Most looked like students. Across the tiny tables with electric candles, they spoke in languages I could not recognize. Tattoos showed on some very prosaic bodies. Pierced lower lips seemed popular. The students tossed down cocktails and laughed at jokes that rang my dullness gong.

The student-comedians ran through their material about professors and exams and favoritism. Then the stage was mine.

Usually stage fright would freeze me. But today had formed a full day.

"I'm on foot patrol in a Flatbush alley at oh-dark-thirty," I said. "And a client type of mine is drinking a 40-ounce bottle of beer in the alley. Anyone breaking the law, I call them 'clients.' No hatred, no rancor. Just police business. Because everyone and everything makes me laugh. All races, creeds, religions. So how can I hate them?"

"I stop. Just watching. I am fascinated. When he set the beer back down, I picked it up without making a sound. He reaches backward to grab it. But his hand cannot find it. He turns around. He sees me in full uniform. What we call, elegantly enough, 'the bag.'"

In the audience, someone snickered. It was hard to tell if he was laughing with me or at me.

"Po-po, police, are punks, yo!" a woman's voice sounded from the back of the café.

That seemed to take care of that.

"My beer-drinking client stares at me in the alleyway, holding his cherished beer. 'I'm a terrible driver,' I tell him, 'so the sergeant wants me to walk.'

'You messing with me because I'm black'

'There's nothing wrong with being black,' I tell him. 'There's a lot of times I wish I could say that I'm not white.'

"'You gonna bust me, man?'

"'I'm a Manhattan Democrat, and I never get between a man and his beer,' I tell him. 'And I would rather have conversation than incarceration. Who is selling guns around here? Who is doing robberies? Give me something and I keep walking."

"'I don't know anything,' he says."

"'Then stand up. Places want us to go to them.'

"'That boy, Marlon, on Winthrop Street, he did that LaundroWorld robbery on Nostrand Avenue last Saturday. He drives a raggedly old red Mustang and keeps his nine gun under the seat somewhere.'

"'Where on Winthrop?' I ask.

"'Third house down off Flatbush. Gray steel door with church stickers on it.'

"My audience, that's how we do what we do," I said. "With his words, I can legally stop Marlon's car, find the gun and put him in a line-up for the robbery."

The audience kept sitting on their hands.

"Is that legal?" a woman's voice finally asked.

"Totally," I said. "This is a college, after all. Let's check with Legal."

"You're making fun of how people talk," a man's voice said.

"Am I?" I asked. "That is how the people on my beat, my beatniks, talk."

"But you're making it into a joke."

"This *is* a comedy open-mike night, right?" I asked.

"He's right," another man said. "Just shut your over-educated face, Carleton."

"It's a serious joke," I said. "Marlon had an excellent chance to blow me right into rock-and-roll heaven when I stopped his car for a traffic violation. I just got to his gun first."

"Dude, leave people alone," the same man said.

That seemed pointless.

"Leave them alone when they rob laundromats?" I asked. "We are after 9/11 now. 9/11 said that cops can be important. But the city still starts us cops off at only $25,000 per year. Grocery workers earn more.

"If you want to gripe to me about us cops, I'll be at the bar here. My mother named me Max. Call me Max. I'll be drinking cheap beer slowly. Because I'm low on capital. And because there's another criminal hurting people right here in this hood. And I need your help to stop him."

Adrenaline laid me low as I squatted down on the barstool.

"Do we have anyone else for open mike night yet?" the barmaid asked.

Nobody answered.

"Man, you should let people drink their beer in peace," a white youngster with a pierced lip slanged up to me.

If I stayed more quiet, this crowd might avoid me.

"Why?" I asked.

Loudsters usually loved their own voices.

"Because that's his right."

"Why do you say that?" I asked.

"Because the law says so," he said.

"Actually, the law says that he cannot drink beer in public," I said. "Why do you think they wrote that law?"

"Racism."

"Classist struggle," another man said, with heavy designer fashion eyewear bobbing down his pug nose. "Written by men who have private places to go and drink."

"You drank beer outdoors as a kid," the first one said. "You're just being hypocritical now. For a paycheck."

"No hypocrite, I," I said. "I slammed beers, gurgled whiskey and lived in a cloud of marijuana smoke as a teenager.

And other drugs. Most of us did. When we age, we see the bigger picture."

"Which is?"

"Do you think that the client in the alley is in control of his own life?" I asked. "Why isn't he drinking at home? Is he nerving himself up for a mugging? Or worse? Would you want your kid sister at 17 walking past that same alley?"

"Now, you're reaching," a woman said from the darkness. Her hair, the color of antique gold, hung braided heavily onto her shoulders. "And your story sounded racist to me."

"Why did it sound racist?" I asked.

"You know," she said.

The crowd seemed to agree and breathe with her.

"No," I said. "I don't know. Let me in on the secret, if you will."

"Because you're a white cop and he's a black man. There's tragic history there."

"I'm not a racist." I said. "So my conscience is clear."

"You're bothering him without any legal right when he's drinking beer."

"Am I?" I asked. "Did you know that more than seventy percent of robbers and rapists do their crimes when they are legally impaired by drugs or drink?"

"I don't believe that," she said. "Are you really a cop?"

I dangled my toes on the bar-stool edge.

"Would you like to see my shield?" I asked.

This was risky. I did not have the real shield anymore. The noble Captain Day was sleeping with it under his pillow.

"No, thank you," she said.

My body sagged.

"It would just depress me," she said. "Oh, you're a cop, all right. Only a New York cop could have that kind of mentality. You said that you need our help here?"

"Yes. This joker broke into a woman's home near here, fondled her sexually and escaped."

I unfolded my sketch and spread it out for them to see.

"Does he look like anyone that you have seen?" I asked.

"Really, Officer?"

"Max."

"Officer. Aren't you reaching a bit?"

"Last stat of this lovely night," I said. "Ninety percent of burglars do their jobs within one mile of their pillows. So he may live near here."

She emerged into the light. Her eyes were heavy-lidded sloe eyes, the color of a coconut, against her slim face. A darkish tone to her skin contrasted with the blonde braids.

"That's a well-crafted sketch," she said.

"Thank you."

"If you really did that, it makes you a kind of Renaissance man."

"Kind of," I said.

"Do you have permission for this kind of thing?" she asked.

"The attack just happened. If I wait for permission, four levels of supervisors will have to play Mesopotamian basketball with One Police Plaza and review my request. By that time, he will attack another woman. One of your neighbors."

"This is a city college," she said. "We can't afford to live here. So she is not our neighbor."

"Please, define the word 'neighbor,'" I said.

"He's got you there, Professor," the first youngster said.

"Professor?" I asked. "What's your name and what, pray tell, do you teach?"

"Professor Jody Quirianna, and what I teach is none of your goddamn business."

"Perhaps not. But this building and college are dedicated to civilization. How do we argue for civilization and ignore women getting brutalized nearby?"

"Well, Officer, I don't think that you're the answer."

"I'm the only answer there is at the moment."

She stepped away, swinging a hand-tooled tan leather book bag behind her. Her boots matched the bag. She wore a clinging dress of darkish green that clung to her strong frame.

"Back to that beer-drinker in the alley," I said. "What if three of his friends join him to reminisce? Might they grow noisy? What if you're trying to sleep and get rested for your Philosophy final ten feet from them?"

"I'd go outside and tell them to shut up."

"Not in Flatbush," I said. "Not in my old precinct."

"Why not?"

"They just might resent you a little bit."

I passed out Xerox copies of my sketch to hands in the darkness.

More questions batted out of the darkness.

I lobbed them back as best that I could.

Professor Jody returned. A CUNY guard, this one with sergeant's stripes and a sideways smashed nose over a wide Latino face, scanned me.

"You a cop?" he said.

"Guilty," I said.

"Shield?"

"Suspended."

"How surprising," Jody said. "I can't imagine why."

"Well, slick, you're not a student here," the guard sergeant said. "So you'll have to cool it out of here tonight. That's college policy."

"Maybe you better tell him not to come back," Jody said. "That's more school policy."

CHAPTER 7.

The next morning, I woke up early.

My to-do list had kept clamoring me awake like a fire bell in the night.

"Good morning, PO Royster," my cellphone voicemail said. "I'm Lieutenant Lenny Hundshamer of CRIT here down at One Police Plaza. Got a couple of quick questions for you. Can you call me back on my direct –"

My thumb mashed that message down. Lieutenant Lenny Whosis of CRIT was not getting a call-back from our hero.

☙

The streets were still dark when I reached the Franklin Hotel on East 87th Street.

I went down the garage ramp.

"Tell all people I love them," Leo said to me. "They teach me to say so at Holy Bible School. Love."

"Yeah, I love you, too." I said.

"God bless," he said.

"If anyone asks about me coming out in uniform, tell them nothing."

"No tell nobody nothing never."

"Leo, your Latin is improving."

"I got enough English to parking their cars," he lisped. His scalp showed through thinning gray hair over his ruddy drinker's face.

"Tell me something," I said. "Why are they so unhappy, when they got everything – custom-made cars, sports clothes, vacations, these regal restaurants here – and nobody around the world has anything?"

Leo grinned his Dickens street-urchin grin.

"They need more loving," he said. "Like us Latins like to give them."

"This is a riddle that I have to figure out," I said.

"Good luck."

"This unhappy neighborhood," I said. "I hang on in my apartment here by rent-control. Can't afford to move. It's the safest neighborhoods in the city. That's why I call it 'the Playpen.' From 59th Street to 86th, from Central Park to the East River, you can live and die inside this area without ever seeing much of real, hairy life."

ଓ

As I thrashed around in the bathroom, putting on my phony uniform, I tried not to think about anything.

You should try it sometime.

Then I stepped back into the garage.

Leo looked me over in my police uniform. The fake silver patrol shield winked on my chest. The cop blues showed creases. I put on the eight-point uniform hat.

"How do I look?" I asked him.

"Is okay," Leo said.

To protect Leo, I could not tell him what I was doing. Stripped and suspended, I was going to patrol the street again in uniform and armed with a toy gun and shield.

"Love," Leo smirked.

"Leo, do you know anything about East 83rd street? Got any buddies there? It's only four blocks away."

"Leo got friends everywhere. I got there, too. What you need?"

"There are different layers to this neighborhood. Not everyone is rich."

"You tell me everything, boss" Leo said. "Don't leave out nothing."

"East 83rd Street has garages like this one," I answered. "And now trendy places like boutiques, nail salons and party stores mix with the older storefront shoeshine spots and Asian drycleaners."

"Until the end of the war in 1945, the neighborhood held mostly Germans, Czechs and Hungarians. In the war, Americans mistrusted Germans. That feeling hurt cafés like the Geiger, the Jaeger House and the Ideal Restaurant. The European population is dying out now or moving away. But sometimes, you still hear the accents."

"They talk funny," Leo said. "Like me."

"Foreign words are still etched into some of the concrete building facades. The older tenement hallways are too narrow to turn a shopping cart around in. Pipes burst in the winter and apartments sizzled in the summer. My apartment is just like them, neglected but in a good neighborhood. Hanging on in one of these buildings myself. Rent control keeps me there.

"The newer buildings brought in the sky-high rents and the younger moneyed crowd. But, after dark, predators still prowl, looking for apartments to crack or drunken Yuppies to rob. So us cops keep it safe. The citizens there should be glad to see me on foot."

"I go talk to my pals there tonight," Leo said. "Whatever you want, I get you."

I left Leo and walked over to East 83rd Street and Third Avenue.

☙

"Good morning, beatnik," I said to a Latino super hauling a pink mattress up from a basement.

He looked at me and threw a quick nod.

Then he dumped the mattress, cussed and went back downstairs.

"They say hello more nicely in the poorer neighborhoods," I said. "They know that they need us flatfoots. Com-Pol is a joke."

My feet turned me down to the tony East End Avenue. A concrete promenade looked out over the river and Hell Gate's Lighthouse. Joggers, dogwalkers and brown-skinned health aides pushing wheelchairs with white-haired, pink-skinned oldsters, filed past.

A blue-and-white NYPD car crested past me on East End Avenue. My feet stopped dead. The black woman passenger cop threw me a wave as she shifted her power-drink bottle over the dashboard.

Trying to look like a real cop, I flicked my head back at her.

That was the smug, all-seeing, all-judging and brief nod that cops always threw each other. It said, "You and I are insiders, wised-up and tough and no boss or citizen better mess with us. We got the gun and shield, and unlimited sick days and the 20-year pension so the world better step off when we trudge by."

A yellow taxi bounced up the block and stopped. A slim woman flowed out and split open her brocade purse to pay.

Something about her triggered my memory.

My feet stepped back. I bumped into the wall.

The woman was Diana, my heartbreak lover of years ago.

She had not aged. She still had the lithe tomboyish body of a teenager.

My eyes wetted.

Short auburn hair framed her face. It was too far to see her eyes but I could remember the large calm blueness of them and the long sweet nights we had spent tumbling and bundling.

A reedy joker in his 40's wearing a short black beard bluejeaned out of the taxi behind her. As his feet touched the asphalt, he started to drift. Any street cop would scan him as trouble, a druggy, a shoplifter or some kind of hustler. He would start bar fights that he could never win.

Diana hooked her fingers into his belt. He stopped drifting. It looked as if she had done it before.

All of me came off that wall to speak with her. Then I stopped.

Diana had left *The Daily News* but she was still a reporter. Her pieces showed up in *New York Magazine, Town and Country* and *Esquire*. She had scored awards for her work.

If she spoke with me, she would know that something was wrong. My voice would give it away. We knew each other that well. She was a better detective than I was. Those magazines fees proved it.

"Bye-bye, Diana," I whispered. "Your cop sources will tell you that I'm stripped and suspended. You'll blow my scheme sky-high and I'll wind up in Bellevue."

So my black patrol sneakers stayed where they were.

"I can't speak with you until I stop the Horn Bug. Then, maybe I'll find you through those magazines."

Obviously, these days, she was off aging chunky cops like me. She had moved on to troubled artistic types.

She mothered this one artist down my block and to a shaky tomorrow.

They turned the corner and were gone.

My belly heaved in and out under the blue uniform.

The Manhattan bittersweets kept rocking me.

Off First Avenue, I stepped into a tiny café named Java Janey's and ordered coffee and a buttered scone from a thickish woman in her thirties. She had pale gray hair and bright squirrely brown eyes. Seeing Diana had jolted me into needing hot food and comfort.

"I'm new here on this beat," I said. "Just feeling my way around. Meeting some of you beatniks."

She nodded. Talking to cops did not come easily to everyone. A lot of people remembered smoking last night's marijuana to get to sleep.

Traffic noise outside filled in the gaps of our conversation.

"We're glad to see you here," she said after a bit.

"You seem like the only one."

"Oh, that's just because everyone here's so self-involved."

The coffee heated my body from the bottom of my feet to my eyelids. The scone tasted homemade.

"You're right about the neighborhood," I said. "My name's Max."

She did not want to say anything. Her eyes skittered away again.

"Pray tell," I said. "What might be your name?"

"Lila."

Finishing the coffee, I paid, tipped and left.

I planned to come back to Java Janey's. Lila was the only person speaking to me today.

☙

A woman jogger, springy brown curls and designer eyewear, walked past me, cooling down.

"Hiya," I said.

She was too cooled down to answer.

"No broken car window glass on the street and no yellow crime-scene tape," I said to her vanishing sweat suit shirt. "No heavy crimes here. But plenty of bad attitude and negative energy."

A chunky Latino man, with an aging silver goatee, cracked open a beer can in a paper bag. He lifted it to his mouth.

"Is that beer for me?" I asked.

He stopped, looked at me and smirked.

"My name's Max. What's yours?"

"Eddie, Officer. I didn't see you there. I wouldn't disrespect you like that."

"I'm sure of that, Eddie. You want to be my good friendly beatnik, right?"

"I'm good and friendly, yeah."

"Me, too," I said.

"I don't want no ticket for the beer. I'll pour it out."

I pretended to think it over.

"That's a good idea, Eddie. Thank you for that."

He poured it in the gutter and walked away before I could change my mind.

"What's a 'beatnik?" he asked someone on the stoop.

Checking the sketch folded inside my uniform hat, I scanned it every time a tall young white type showed up. My suspect, the Horn Bug, was ankling around here somewhere. But these locals would not put the finger on him for me.

My toy radio stayed dumb.

In the pants pocket alongside it, my phone kept playing the real police calls.

To make it look good, I scribbled some nonsense in my memo book. But nobody reacted. In the slums, everyone with a car worries and catcalls you, thinking you might be writing a summons on their family ride. But, here, everyone seemed resigned to getting a ticket for something or other.

I noted some potholes in the asphalt and thought about calling the Department of Trans to fill them in.

I got the feeling that nobody would thank me for it.

My shoulders drooping, I trudged back to Leo's garage, changed out of uniform and walked across the park to the 24th Precinct at West 100th Street.

I phoned Manhattan North Homicide and asked for Sgt. Lipkin.

☙

Ten minutes later, Lipkin came into Central Park where I sat on the bench. A slight elf of a man with sandy hair and a broken nose, he always dressed in crisp dark suits and pure white shirts to balance the chaos that permeated his world of murders.

"Did you dry-clean yourself?" I asked.

"Don't worry. Nobody's following me. Are you going paranoid on me, Maxy?"

With my voice cracking, I told him about everything except my fake patrol in uniform.

"Listen to your lawyer," he said. "Take the cure. Go inside and let him duke it out in court."

I sighed and sagged against the wooden slats.

"That's your best advice?" I asked.

I could hear the nerves speeding up my own voice.

"Your Captain Day is right," Lipkin said. "If you catch this Horn Bug, Day cannot sling you into the Home for the Bewildered. You can trust him there."

"Can you make sure of that?"

"Sure. When the Commissioner gets back from vacation. After Labor Day. I helped him years ago. So he'll hear me out about you. Even though I'm just a sergeant."

"Thanks, Al."

"Until then, Drezek is in charge and he is the bought dog of One Police Plaza. Drezek will do anything to avoid controversy. If your captain says to lock you down in a nut-house, Drezek will bury you. All he cares about is becoming the next Commissioner."

This was getting worse. My knees twitched towards each other.

"You'll help me run a lead or two?" I asked.

"Can't. After Sunday I'm going off on sick leave, for tests. Irregular heartbeat, chest pains and that stuff. I'm afraid that you're on your own."

CHAPTER 8.

Feeling like a ten-year-old approaching his school principal, I knocked on the brownstone door where the Horn Bug had done his Horn Buggery.

The socialite woman opened the door.

Her model's face congealed. She looked like a pampered animal in a silk bathrobe, no makeup on her face. Her slim long-legged body crouched in the doorway. Wisps of hair moved as she shook her head.

"What are you bothering me for?" she asked.

"That's a good question," I said. "You may have the advantage of me there."

"If I want it."

"I came because I wanted to see how you are."

"I've got plenty of people asking me that. Better qualified than you. Your Captain Day called to apologize and offer his help."

"I bet."

"Wisecracking won't help you. He said that you have always been a problem and does not know why they haven't booted you off the force. You think that you know more than anyone else and go off on wild tangents."

"If he only knew."

"So, please do not come around here. Those detectives from the Internal Affairs said that you might threaten me to drop the complaint and they left me their cards, with clear instructions on what to do."

This was getting into choppy waters. I shook my head like I used to when left hooks rattled my head bones.

"I came to apologize," I said. "What you suffered was something that nobody should have to."

"Because of your bumbling. My husband is coming home from Singapore next week, and I will tell him all about this mess. I didn't want to call him and ruin his business meeting. If he heard of this, he would swim back here and knock you down as soon as he dried off."

I tried not to think about Manhattan State Hospital's windows with their criminal-small wire windows looking out on a dumpster. Having taken many psychos there, I had checked out the accommodations.

"I became a cop to stop things like that happening to you," I said. "That's all that I can offer."

"Then you failed. How does it feel to be a failure?"

I let that hang and ripen the air.

"Everything about that night terrifies me. His hands on me. Where he touched me. My husband and I enjoy a happy marriage and I'm going to keep it that way. When he gets back, he and I will talk about that night."

"May we talk about that now?"

"Not with you."

"My name is Max."

"The most sickening thing about that night was not him but you. This great police department cannot watch a house and prepare to catch one person in that house. That sickens me, literally. My gout flared up. I've had the flu since that night and it feels like I will never get better."

"I have it all the time," I said. "From stress. I just want two minutes of your time to explain things."

"Then please wait here," she said.

She closed the door and locked it.

"That says a lot about how she trusts cops," I said aloud.

Neighbors went by me.

My clothes were a loose tan T-shirt, blue jeans and the same black sneakers, buffed shiny for patrol. I did not look like anyone's idea of a power broker, standing in the doorway.

She opened the door.

"You won't leave," she said. "So I called those detectives from your Internal Affairs team or whatever it is called. The ones who spank you. They told me that the captain had taken your gun and badge but that you were still unstable and dangerous. They are sending cars now."

My shoulders hunched like I was taking a right cross to the face. I ducked my head down and spoke quickly, voice breaking.

"Goodbye," I said. "I hope that you will feel better soon."

I turned on my heel and walked away from the townhouse.

A blue-and-white RMP turned the corner and headed down the street towards me. Internal Affairs must have called Communications and whistled up a car to protect this woman from drooling crazy Max Royster.

"This looks un-good," I said aloud.

The cops inside the car were squinting at me.

I went across the street and slowly mounted the steps to another brownstone. I wanted to look like a homeowner returning to his abode.

My hand shook as I fumbled my own house keys out.

Burglars used this trick when they felt someone watching them. Nobody cared about someone coming back to his own home.

Manhattan felt like a wide flat frying pan, and I was the cockroach scuttling across it and getting cooked.

Everyone's eyes felt like they were burning across my shoulder blades.

If the cops sniffed and stopped me, they could lock me up for Witness Tampering or Obstruction of Governmental Administration. All kinds of charges, some of which they probably had not even invented yet.

"Oh, mama" I chanted to myself. "If I only had my youth again."

My heart hammered.

If I collapsed now, any cops would find the toy shield and gun on me.

That would put me in a straitjacket right quickly. Bellevue Hospital would carve up a fresh young turkey for my orientation dinner among the new room-mates.

My eyes squooshed shut.

That probably would not help things.

My nerved fingers dropped the keys at my own feet.

I was still bumbling and fumbling through life.

Scooping down to snag them, I said some raucous words. That was my try at Method Acting.

The sound of car doors slamming and handcuffs ratcheting would loud up this quiet street.

But nothing happened.

When I screwed up my courage to open my eyes, the cops were gone. The street roiled just like before.

They had just given the block a quick glance and kept rolling along. The shrewd veterans would use the extra ten minutes for coffee and a slice before radioing that they were clear for another job.

CHAPTER 9.

Two hours later, I came back to the victim's brownstone and knuckled the door again.

She opened it.

Her face flamed.

"Are you deranged?" she asked.

"I have what you need here. 'Sopa de Gallego,' imported by Lexington Avenue bus from Spanish Harlem. Ancient Castilian remedy for the common cold."

"I can call those Internal Affairs gentlemen again."

"Will they bring you soup?"

"Do you think that this is funny?"

"Tragicomic."

"Please leave."

"I'll leave you the soup. And aspirin from you're your local pill-roller pharmacy. Plus Cure-a-Flu. I swear by Cure-a-Flu. And there's some natural healing herbs from the nutrition place on Lex. Can I interest you in walking to the park for some sunshine and better air? That beats drugs."

"I told you that I can barely walk."

"But how does it sound? Tempting, right?"

"I would rather be alone," she said.

"Like Greta Garbo. I am a strong police-type. I could carry you."

"That does paint a picture."

"Do you have a wheelchair lying around? I could wheel you to the park."

"Nobody normal uses a wheelchair for the flu. The neighbors would think that I'm dying."

"Not if you wiggled your toes at them."

"Droll."

"You claim to have gout."

"Oh, I have it, all right."

"That explains the wheelchair."

She hung in her doorway, thinking it over and making faces.

"If anybody cares," I said.

"I told you that I'm well married and happy."

"What has that to do with wheeling you to the park to recover on a sunny day?"

"Mister Cop –"

"Max."

"Mister Cop, I grew up in this neighborhood and have many close friends to bring me outside, if needed. I certainly don't need an irrational stranger for company. I can do it myself."

"Call them, then," I said. "But remember those answering machines that vexed you before. I bet that your pals are still busy. In this Playpen, 'busy' is their favorite four-letter word."

She looked past me, maybe for witnesses.

"The wheelchair is in the basement, if you don't mind bringing it up," she said. "I bought it after a skiing accident. Give me a few minutes to get better dressed."

☙

Central Park hung in the afternoon heat.

"My first name is Elspeth," she said.

"Pretty name."

"And I still intend to follow through with the complaint against you."

"Absolutely."

"Don't you care?"

"What jobs have you worked at, on life's great stage?"

"None like yours, that's true."

"Then it's hard to explain."

I wheeled her down the hilly path and then over to the Sheep Meadow. Something tugged at my senses. I could not put a name to it.

"I won't bore you with that jazz about us dying in gun battles," I said. "That rarely happens. But policing is a punishment-centered bureaucracy. When you're on patrol, there is a black cloud that follows you. And, every day, it gets closer."

"I don't understand."

"You're not missing a thing."

The disco roller-skater crowd swooped and caterwauled nearby us. A wispy man who looked about seventy took off his T-shirt to display a bony tanned body. His red-and-white-checkered pants read "Sex, It's The Real Thing."

"Has anyone come to your brownstone lately, to install or fix anything?"

"You think that the burglar was looking me over?"

"The smart ones do."

"That scares me."

Her fine exquisite eyes worried now. They hopscotched around us. I sensed an opening.

"What else scares you, Elspeth?"

"Well, it's hard to verbalize."

I tried to soften my tone and every other aspect about myself.

"Try, please."

"Well, if I am afraid, then the logical thing to do is call the police. And not to complain about one of them. Like I'm doing about you."

"So you feel conflicted," I said. "Because the only thing between you and that attacker, that deviate, is me."

"Are you so special?"

"I'm different. I believe that a cop on patrol can inspire civilians to help him prevent crimes. Without fancy and useless Community Policing fakery. I've done it. And I've seen it work with the few other cops who try it."

"Why don't more officers try it that way?" she asked.

"Because it means reaching out, taking social and professional risks, being patient and not caring if your partners mock you."

"Policemen are not that afraid," she said.

"Socially, we are. Most of us are sharply aware that we are making $25,000 a year to start. In a city where you need about $70,000 to have a comfortable family life."

"And that makes you all afraid?"

"Shy. Unless cops are drunk or trying to seduce you or to arrest you, they feel that they have little of interest to say. I call 'Royster's Law'."

"I don't recall anyone coming near my home to look me over."

"Do you usually go out during the day?"

"In this icky heat? Not unless I have to."

Nobody seemed to be watching us. But something kept making me whip my head around.

"How are you feeling now?" I asked.

"Much better, thank you. But nothing's changed my opinion of you as an officer. It's not the right fit for you.
How long have you done it?"

"Just a few years."

"But I thought that you had to be young to join the police."

"It's a long story," I said.

"What else have you worked at?"

"Schoolteacher, print reporter, chef, merchant seaman, bookseller –"

"Stop it," she said. "You're joking, of course."

"You should see my resume."

"You should get out of policing before you get hurt."

We were pushing by the East Drive, near the rowboat lake. The bushes rustled behind me.

I stopped pushing the chair and lunged behind and into the bushes.

"Max, don't do that!"

Something thick thumped my head. I staggered.

It was a low tree branch. I had run smack into it with my forehead. I groped it with my hand and said a harsh and terrible word. Tears stung my eyes.

My hands formed into fists. I snapped my head lower and crouched.

Four high-school kids lay humped inside the bushes. They rested their heads on their schoolbooks. One had a tiny pile of marijuana spread out over his binder. A pack of rolling papers lay alongside. I smelled sweat and plastic binders but no marijuana smell. Not yet.

Nobody looked like the Horn Bug.

I blew out a breath and tried to quiet my hands.

"Hey!" the smallest one said, a pasty-faced teenager with thick health-plan eyeglasses. "What's your problem, dude?"

"Shell-shock," I said. "Maybe Cholera Morbis."

"Get out of here! Some kind of freak!"

"We'll call the cops!"

"That would be redundant," I said. "So long, younger generation."

Rubbing the bruise I could feel rising on my forehead, I came back to where Elspeth was scanning me as if I were already inside the asylum. Her face paled under the light day-in-the-park makeup.

"What are you doing?" she asked. "Scaring me for no reason and terrifying those children? You don't belong in police work, that's clear. And that's what I will tell my lawyer to tell your bosses. It's time for you to go."

CHAPTER 10.

The next morning, sadness hung over me like a blackout curtain.

Rain tattooed my windows.

"Police Officer Royster, this is Lieutenant Lenny Hundshamer of CRIT."

"Am I having a nightmare?" I mumbled.

"I need to just ask a few quick questions," the high scratchy voice went on.

It was coming from my phone.

"Nothing serious," he went on. "CRIT works with Internal from time to time. What time is good for me to stop by?"

That did it. "Internal" was boss-speak for "Internal Affairs," who harvested citizen complaints and threshed cops into mulch with them.

I squished one of my Kaufman's Military Surplus pillows on top of the phone. The muslin muffled Lieutenant Lenny's voice.

Then I pitched myself back into the Land of Nod.

"No reason to wake up today," I whispered sometime later.

ↀ

When I did roll up out of bed, the rainy windows showed night.

"Our hero needs to quell these blues," I said aloud. "There is bourbon or the ballroom for that."

Nobody answered. That was lucky.

Tomorrow, I might start hearing voices.

"Ballroom it is."

Moving through the studio apartment that cost me three weeks pay, I dressed in a loose, dark shirt, black jeans and light Italian ankle boots for spinning on the dance floor. Leaving my wallet on the bed, I shucked the loose greens into my hip pocket.

My fake stuff stayed in my hiding place inside a trash bag in the kitchen. Whatever CRIT was, they might come toe-dancing up the stairs to search my place with a warrant. Those toys would sink me.

Lipkin's voice gruffed up when he answered my phone call. "Stay away from CRIT," he said.

There were those four initials again.

"They are the slimiest squad in Internal Affairs."

Coming from Lipkin, I did consider being intimidated.

"Powerful name."

"CRIT investigated me for telling a suspect to shut up. That's a violation of the Patrol Manual, they said. I asked them if they were serious. Two of those snakes said, 'Sergeant Lipkin, we'll put you under oath in the Trial Room. If you're found to be lying about telling this suspect to shut up, you could be dismissed.'"

"Dismiss their mother," I said.

"Then they said, 'Well, Sarge, you've practically admitted saying it.'

"I told them 'This suspect kicked and spat on me in the Interrogation Room and then tried to grab my gun. He had practically beheaded his neighbor for playing the TV too loud. How do you think I remember what I said after what, ten months ago?'

"Then I lost six vacation days for being uncooperative in their witch hunt. Don't say hello to them without you got a lawyer at your hip."

"You're talking to the right man."

"Maxy, what's your plan?"

"Told you. I gotta catch me the Horn Bug."

"Grow up, junior. You've been watching too many movies."

"That's my only way clear of this goat rodeo."

Folding up my phone, I kept my apartment lights on and left.

☙

My feet padded up the stairs to the rooftop. I used my roof key to unlock the door and stepped out onto it.

Pools of rainwater slicked the tar.

A huge whitish gray lump of cloud hung overhead.

From years in the building, I knew the territory.

Six feet of space separated my building from the next. I squinted at the next roof.

"I hope nothing changed over there," I whispered. "Don't look down. I can see the headlines in *The Post*. 'Despondent, Cuckoo Cop in Suicide Leap.'"

I leapt.

My feet lit on the other roof. I landed and stayed on my feet.

I blew out a breath.

"Stop CRIT," I said. "Stop the police state."

At Christmas time, I had done favors and bought drinks for the supers on the block until they trusted me with spare keys in case I got locked out.

I fitted a key to the other roof door. It worked.

So much for security.

I went inside, locked it behind me and moved downstairs.

The service entrance opened onto East 93rd Street.

Some CRITter might be staking out my place. Maybe the vaunted Lieutenant Lenny Hundshamer himself was eagle-eying my windows, ready to pounce.

"Hell of a way for a boulevardier like myself to have to live," I muttered.

☙

Down the block, a car door opened. Something dropped onto the asphalt. It sounded wet.

I froze.

Moving could draw attention.

I knew these tricks from my own stakeouts.

Then the door shut.

Someone was sitting in a parked car.

It could be Harry K. Thaw with a 1911 revolver crouching to redeem his marriage by shooting Stanford White. But I doubted it.

More likely, a clutch of unprincipled varlets, broken men of CRIT, with no conscience anymore, were ready to stuff marijuana or French postcards into my jeans hip pocket and swear that they found it there.

The City would save millions in health and pension costs by firing me.

It was a good time to slither.

So I slithered along doorways, against the traffic direction.

That way, CRIT would have to tail me on foot or loop around corners, making them easier to see.

Nobody moved after me on the block.

I wondered again who might be in that parked car and what they were doing.

It would stay another of my unsolved Playpen mysteries.

First Avenue ran northbound so I walked south, looking for the surveillance men that cops call "pavement artists."

Nobody appeared out from the crowded sidewalks.

I kept walking.

☙

I reached Hunter College.

A sad-faced Campus Peace Officer in a dark blue uniform was inside the 68th Street entrance of Hunter College. He motioned me over to his podium.

It was time to go on the offensive.

"Evening, officer," I said. "PO Royster from the One-Nine Precinct. We met before. Remember that Russian kid who was throwing up from drinking too much?"

I was winging it, lying through my teeth.

"Think so," he said. "So much goes down here."

"How true." I said. "When does Professor Jody Quirianna finish her class? I've got to give her a property receipt before she has a coronary."

"Yeah. I hear you."

We men silently reflected for a beat about women and their moods.

"The schedules are all locked up in the day shift," he said.

"Supposed to be around nine," I said. "Don't you usually see her now?"

"Depends. I don't know all the teachers yet."

"Then I'll cool it outside. Thanks for your help."

I sank down outside on one of the stone benches, out of his line of sight. Waiting here like a kid felt silly and high-schoolish but it also felt right. I remembered how her smile smoothed the slim planes of her face.

Another surveillance trick was sinking into the concrete.

I tried that now, breathing in deeply to relax.

Students passed.

So did time.

Greenish buses wheezed past me on Lexington Avenue.

"Puppy love lasts long," I sang off-key to myself against the bus garrumphing past. "This is in-fat-ua-tion."

Then she appeared, in a soft brown Australian duster with epaulets and brass fittings. It matched her strong outdoor frame.

"Good evening, professor," I said, with my most winning smile.

She stopped and looked me over.

"What is this?" she asked.

"This is in-fat-ua-tion," I recited from memory.

"I'm not the least bit infatuated."

"How can you be so sure?"

"And I ask you not to be, either," she said. "Now good evening. I've suffered through a long day."

"Yes, and I agree with you."

"So do I. Goodnight."

She moved away.

Using what was left of my thigh muscles, I moved towards her again.

"On the other hand," I said. "There is tango, appetizing food and a cocktail to relax one."

"No, thank you."

"Then we slump back alone to our tawdry apartments to make sure that nobody lifted our furniture."

"What makes you think that I want to dance?"

"Everyone does. Because dancing is enchanting."

"Not when I try it."

"The woman just has to follow the man."

"I don't do following."

"Only on the floor. After that, we both know that women rule."

"Why would I want to dance with you?"

"The café is closer than the subway station," I said.

"The subway station is beneath our feet," she retorted.

"I was speaking spiritually."

"You say that the food is good?"

"Sublime."

"Then we'll try it. Spiritually."

CHAPTER 11.

Sessions 73 Café held up a corner on First Avenue, a wooden dance floor inside and a balcony outside. Argentine tango dancers swirled around the floor to an edgy violin ballad.

Jody put her purse and schoolgirl book bag near a free table. We sat. An emaciated young waitress with a Slavic accent took her order for Maryland crab cakes, a cheese plate and white wine. I ordered a glass of champagne to cut the dust.

Then I stood up, and we stepped onto the dance floor.

Her body felt athletic and tensile in my arms. A deep cleft down her spine tickled my fingertips.

"I don't know how to do this," she said.

"That's okay."

"Why?"

"Because this Argentine Tango is the most frustratingly elusive dance in the world."

"Meaning what?" she asked.

"Spiritual."

"How so?"

"Because there are no set steps. No real diagrams on where to put your feet. In order to learn it, you must take many lessons over a period of years."

"And you've taken lessons?"

"Not yet," I said. "They're quite pricey."

"Then what are we doing?"

"Moving to the music. For us without lots of cash, some call that dancing."

She followed closely, feeling every shift of my body.

Aline, my sometime dancing partner, whirled past me with a man partner. He was a slim young businessman type in a flawless black suit. She looked happier than I remembered her. Maybe they were in love.

"Hello, Max," Aline said. "Good to see you dancing again. You've been away."

Her partner did not look cheery about this greeting.

"That's right," I said. "Been working."

"Working at what?"

"Working at not going away," I said. "Far away."

Aline giggled. Her partner spun her into a complex step where she rubbed her calf against his.

Jody looked at me with disapproval.

"You would enjoy a dance that is frustratingly elusive," Jody said. "I had asked you about your life and you eluded me."

"Oh, dear. The awful truth."

"Stop clowning."

"I could be anything you want. A lifeguard in a car wash."

"Max."

Hearing her speak my name intrigued me.

Her voice held the burr of a city accent but she chose words like a reader of books.

"Time for truth on a dance floor?" I asked.

"What do you think?"

"Most people lie until they get into bed."

"Then they really start lying," she said.

I looked around the floor and wondered if she would walk away before eating her crab cakes.

"Here goes the truth," I said. My voice dipped under the violins. "I'm suspended, no gun or shield, about to be forced into a mental hospital for instability."

She stopped dancing and looked me up and down.

"For how long?" she asked.

"Maybe forever."

"Why? Did you kill someone?"

"Only my own career."

"What did you do?"

"Followed my heart."

"And?"

"I spoke truth to power."

The dance ended.

"That's not a real strong selling point, your auto - biography," she said.

"Not in these parlous times, no. But I am cute and fun."

A shudder seemed to run through her.

"After that, I need a drink," she said.

"That's the idea of the week."

We sat. The starving Slav, who moved like a ballerina brought us *un petit* snack.

"You've been a policeman for a long time?"

"A few hard-fought, disorganized and inconclusive years. With many punishments and suspensions."

"Why don't you resign?"

"At this point, they won't let me. It's a mandatory commitment under the state health law."

"Then leave the city."

"They will put a felony warrant on me for Reckless Endangerment. And Official Misconduct. They extradite ex-cops from anywhere. Because we are supposed to be better than the regular fools."

"That seems very harsh."

"The Department is very harsh," I said. "In matters of discipline, they are 19th century horse soldiers when it comes to spanking us naughty boys."

"But cops don't seem worried."

"Because the Department lets us get fat and shout bad words across alleyways. But they are always ready to yank down our britches and chastise us in public."

"I think that you're sugarcoating it," she said. "You must have hurt someone."

"Only myself."

We ate.

Some of the dancers moved with grace and speed. The men would shift weight, wait for their partner and then swirl forward again. Aline had improved her steps. Maybe the businessman was teaching her the tango.

We danced again.

This time, she let her body follow the music.

"Tomorrow is literally a school day for me," she said.

"Then shall we be off?"

"I can get a taxi home outside," she said.

"Where is home?"

"Home is Harlem. As an investment, I signed my life away on a brownstone that I can never afford."

I paid and we went outside onto First Avenue. My ankle bones crackled from dancing. Tomorrow, I would feel it getting up.

I was in no shape for a psych ward full of confused weightlifters. They would eat me up.

"Royster!" someone shouted from across First Avenue. "Stand fast!"

"Who is that?" Jody asked.

"My past indiscretions," I said.

The someone was a whittled woodchip of a man, whitish hair showing scalp on top, jowls and dewlaps flapping, waving arms and making faces at me. His expensive dark suit draped around him.

"That must be Lieutenant Lenny Hundshamer of CRIT," I said.

"Crit? What planet is that? Is he some science fiction monster?" she asked.

"Royster! I have to talk with you!"

"Let's go," I said to Jody. "Rapidly."

Lieutenant Lenny tried springing across traffic. But the First Avenue traffic had other ideas. A yellow cab airbrushed him back onto the curb. He tried again. But his sprinting days were long past. More of New York blocked him.

The light changed.

A bus rattled between us. Some of the windows were open. I grabbed Jody's purse. She pulled it back. I looped the purse strap around my neck, took the book bag from her and jammed my left wrist through the handle.

"Jump!" I shouted. "Catch onto the bus window ledge!"

"What?"

"Hook your hand there!"

She leaped up. Her hands caught the edge of the open window and held on. She brought her knees up to brace them against the bus.

I jumped. It was only three feet above my head.

My hands slapped the window ledge and held. Back muscles clenched.

Pedestrians stared at us.

Car horns honked.

The bus lurched uptown, carrying us like twin bobbles bouncing on the side.

"We'll be killed!" Jody shouted, giggling.

"Naw. We kids did it all the time. Called it 'skitching.' Nobody got hurt."

"It's a good thing that I'm a rock-climber," she said.

Lieutenant Lenny stood in the middle of the avenue. He spun around, looking for us.

"Royster!" he shouted. "Where are you? I'll find you!"

The bus stopped and then kept going.

The lieutenant got smaller.

Jody's eyes heated up in her smooth face. She looked more excited and alive than ever before. A wisp of bronze hair blew into her rosebud mouth but she tongued it back out.

Headlights lit up her face again.

"This is a beautifully goddamn unforgettable first date," she whispered.

ଓ

The bus lurched, then stopped.

Jody and I swung like marionettes.

She dropped.

Her legs splayed out and she landed balanced on both feet. I blew out a relief breath. Ballet or gymnasium training showed.

The bus stayed stopped.

"Police officer!" Lieutenant Lenny crowed from the street in front of the bus. He stood there, gold lieutenant's shield dangling in his left hand while the right showed his hip holster.

"Man, I could just run you right over," the tired-out, black bus driver wheezed from behind the wheel. "You must be crazy."

Lenny strode back to us.

"Royster, get down here!" he shouted. "Playing boy-ass games. You're still in the Department."

I dropped next to Jody.

Lenny frisked me rough. He did a thorough job.

"What's the Probable Cause for this, Lieu?" I asked.

"Shut up or I'll frisk her, too."

"I'm leaving," Jody said. She looked shaken by this Storm Trooper routine.

"You can't," Lenny said.

"Why not?" I asked. "If you suspect her of a crime, then name it right now. Or she can leave. That's the law."

"Don't worry, Max," Jody said. "I'm going to report him."

"You can't," I said. "He is Internal Affairs."

"CRIT," Lenny corrected me.

"Man, can I move my bus?" the driver shouted from his window. "Since you all are friends and everything."

"Not yet," Lenny said.

The driver said something unregenerate about Lenny and gunned the engine. The bus whooshed away from us. The other riders made faces as they gawked through the windows.

Lenny showed his shield to the traffic sluicing around us.

A gray Taurus stopped. The driver squinted at us three, the unlikely trio.

"Police emergency," Lenny said. "I need your car."

"What emergency?" I said. "Don't listen to him, pal. He's just cuckoo. Rat run wild."

"Okay, officer," the driver, a born follower in a Mets T-shirt and purplish printed shorts said, scratching himself. "Whatever you say."

"How come I never find these cooperative types when I'm working?" I asked.

"Where do I get it back?" the driver asked.

"19th Precinct," Lenny said. "On Six-seven Street, off Lex. Get in, you two."

"Why?" Jody asked.

"Or else I arrest you for Obstructing Governmental Administration," he said. "Cuff you, throw you in a cell with whores, and you don't see a judge for three days of hell."

"Is that right?" she asked me.

"It ain't right," I replied, "but it's true."

"Spare me the epigrams," she said, getting in the back. "This is the last time I ever tango with a policeman."

"I imagine it is," I said.

Lenny drove us across to Second Avenue and then downtown.

My breath came in short. My thumbs twitched against my palms. This felt all wrong. My suspicions started cork-screwing around.

"We going to the precinct?" I asked.

I wanted that. The precinct was big, loud, sloppy and open. It was everything that Lenny was not.

He did not answer.

That worried me more.

CHAPTER 12.

Lenny pulled up near Elspeth's brownstone and parked at a fireplug. Lenny did not care about much.

He got out, still not speaking, and led us to her brownstone.

"What's this all about?" Jody asked.

Lenny shook his head.

He motioned me to the door.

I rang the bell.

Nothing happened.

He motioned for me to open the door.

I shook my head.

He stepped forward, grasped my belt and pushed the door open. Then he hauled me inside the brownstone.

"This is illegal, Lieu," I said. Nerves gacked my voice higher. "You can't just do this."

He switched on the hall lights and brought me to the staircase.

We went upstairs, past the living room. Oil paintings of tycoons and patriarchs stared dismissively down at us.

On the third floor, I smelled perfume.

He bulled me inside a bedroom.

Elspeth lay sprawled on a four-poster bed. Her naked body shone in the lamplight. Her face was purpled, dead, with a nylon stocking knotted around her throat. Bruises on her smooth thighs showed rape.

"Awwww!" Jody sounded behind us.

"This is what your new boyfriend just did, Lady Citizen," Lenny said. "Are you going to help him get away with it?"

I spun him around and grabbed his lapels, primed to head-butt and drop him.

"Go ahead, Royster," he breathed. He smelled of Bay Rum and shrimp scampi. "An assault charge is all I need."

"That's right." I said, to break the rage spasm. I dropped my hands and stepped away.

"How did you do it, Lieu?" I asked. "Get the M.E. and his guys away from here? Along with the other detectives and uniforms and bosses? A sex killing on this block means big press."

He shrugged and sneered at me.

Jody started weeping.

I kept staring.

"I get it," I said. "You did not tell anyone. Not yet. You found her dead and left her here alone. That's violating every rule in the Patrol Manual for coming upon a Deceased Person. The killer could have still been hiding in this castle."

"I checked," Lenny said.

"Alone? That took guts. But maybe he slipped out behind you. You let him slide out just to come looking for me in the tango place. You had tailed me there before. The regular dancers said that I would be there."

Lenny drew us back outside the brownstone.

ଓ

"I can't handle this," Jody said, her eyes wide at the slamming doors and radio squawks from the street.

"I didn't kill anyone," I assured her.

"That's not it. Right now, I just have to avoid any kind of controversy. Like this murder."

"Why is that?" he asked.

"Don't answer that," I said.

"You're giving legal advice, Royster? I've got a block of richies who saw you arguing with Elspeth. And a 911 run on tape about you harassing her. If she drops the complaint, then you can go back to doing what kooks like you do on Madison Avenue and 66th Street."

"It's best if I talk to you?" Jody asked him.

"Don't talk to him without a lawyer," I said.

"Royster, would you like a collar for Obstructing Governmental Administration?"

"Oh, naked fear. Jody, you're not a suspect. He cannot hold you. Go home, please."

"Don't do that," Lenny said. "You might force me to do something drastic right now, with you and your boyfriend here."

"We're trying to help you," Jody wailed.

"Then you better come clean with me now. Or else tonight will warp the rest of your life."

"Jody, he's bluffing. Us cops do this three times a day, after meals."

Jody paled under her high color.

"I don't know," she wailed.

"Miss, your boyfriend's going down –"

"He's not my boyfriend! He never will be."

My feet stepped back. I shook my head, feeling the fear-sweat.

"Then don't ruin yourself. Talk to me. Help me clear up who butchered that good woman back there."

I swallowed hard, knowing what might happen.

More detective cars drove towards us on the street.

"Lieu, let her slide, and I'll talk to you," I said. "No lawyering up. Two cops talking."

He squinted at me. Behind the tinted blue glasses, his eyes fandagoed around. He worked his right hand and shook it. Scars and lumps showed on the hand.

Something had once chewed his hand and spat it back out.

"How do I know that you'll do that once she leaves?" he asked.

I swallowed. It was getting harder to do.

"My word," I said.

He snorted. Then he nodded his bristly gray head.

"Okay," he said. "Miss, you give your information to my guy over there, in the police jacket. Everything current or else you're in worse trouble. Show him your ID."

She nodded. Tears scored lines down her face. Slim legs showed as she moved to the side of the brownstone.

A preppy-looking black detective kept ogling her as he asked her questions.

"Lieutenant, I'm all wrong for this," I said. "My contact with Elspeth is all documented in that Unusual Incident Report the night of the burglary. Why should I kill her?"

"Why did you come here and talk to her?"

"To apologize for what happened."

"Did she accept it?"

"Would most civilians?"

"How did that make you feel, Royster?"

"Sad."

"Whenever I feel sad, I try fixing it. How did you try fixing it?"

"I didn't," I said. "It feels worse now."

"You're an idealistic type, right? Don't bother to answer. I've gone over your jacket already. And your application to the Job."

"CRIT gets everything, huh?"

"Merchant seaman, Hong Kong chef, unemployed for long periods of time, bookseller, a middle-aged roustabout who fell onto this Job at the age of 42. How did you swing that when the cut-off age is 35?"

"They thought me cute and fun."

"Well, I don't. To me, you're a spoiled brat raised and schooled around these richies. You got their manners but not their cash. That hacks you off. Because you think that you're better than they are."

"Everyone thinks that they're better than the next fool on that green subway seat," I said.

"I think that you brooded about it and came back to do something about it. She objected. You saw that you were in worse trouble. You snapped. She was a snob, right? Who was she to ruin your career?"

"Your theory is a lot of petrified apple butter," I said. "Nothing can ruin my career."

Up and down the block, brownstone windows opened. Neighbors who had known Elspeth craned their heads out to see different blue-and-white police cars pull up. Crime Scene Unit cars emptied out.

Lenny's right hand twitched. It opened and closed.

He shook it and kneaded the skin. His eyes closed. He opened a pill jar from his side jacket pocket and took two.

"Lieu, what the hell happened to your hand?"

"Nothing."

"That 'nothing' looks pretty painful."

"Forget that," he said. "Trying to distract me."

The scent of Bay Rum from his white-on-white shirt grew stronger to my nose. My question was making him sweat.

"Wasn't trying that at all," I said.

"This gets us nowhere fast," he said. "Get in my car, Royster. We're taking a little ride."

"For what?" I asked.

Nerves fluttered my voice.

"Because you're still a Member of the Service and I'm a lieutenant."

"But I'm suspended. Does that mean that I have to obey?"

He seized me before the words left my mouth. I dodged left.

He forced me back against his car and ran a quick rough frisk across my belt-line.

"Nice grip," I said. "Why not try it on crooks?"

"Why not crooked cops?" he asked. "Get in now. Or I handcuff you and we play it that way."

I sat down in the back seat.

He muttered to some of the detective bosses unfolding from the dark blue Chevy Monte Carlos that the Job favored. The bosses gaped at me inside the car and nodded.

"This rasps my worries worser," I said aloud. "Looks like Lieutenant Lenny is in charge, and the bosses are kneeling to him. That does not look good for our hero."

He slammed his way back into the car. We started driving away.

☙

My feet drummed the floor.

If we were heading towards Bellevue, I was going to bolt out of the car. No way was I going gentle into that good night.

The door latch felt cold against my sweaty palm.

"It's a good time to get this done, Max," he said.

We both thought that one over.

"Meaning what, Lieutenant?" I asked.

"Settle this once and for all. And then get a good night's sleep."

"You've got a wild imagination," I said. "I did not hurt anyone ever the way that Elspeth was hurt tonight."

"So let's make it right together."

I shut up. Lenny was too shrewd a detective for me to play word games with him.

We reached 67th Street. The street was jam-packed with blue-and-whites and Department of Transportation traffic vans that we nicknamed "Dotties." The 19th Precinct, the oldest precinct house still standing, its red terra-cotta brickwork dating from 1887, loomed over both of us.

"Royster, what the hell are you doing to wreck my precinct?" Captain Day asked, coming out of a green Toyota at the curb.

Day sported a poplin sports jacket with his gold captain's shield clipped to the breast pocket. Bristle poked through his cheeks. Red rimmed his eyes.

"Cap, get some sleep," I said. "You look worse than I do. The loneliness of command."

"Royster, you'd screw around at your own funeral."

"Why not? Perfect place."

"Champ, who are you?" Day asked Lenny.

Day scanned Lenny and his climber-up-the-ladder business suit. His expression made it obvious he did not care what the answer was.

"Lieutenant Hundshamer, CRIT. Your whiffle ball, Royster, here is a murder suspect now."

"Shoot who?" I asked.

"Hundshamer, I heard about you," Day said. "How's your hand?"

"Is that supposed to be funny?"

"Take it as you like."

"Oh, golly, the adults are a-fussing in front of me," I said.

"Is Royster under arrest?" Day asked.

"Making steady progress that way."

"Under arrest now? Remember that a false statement to a superior officer can get you fired."

"I don't see any officer around here who is very superior," he said. "And I don't need the Manual read to me."

"If Royster is not being detained or arrested, he walks right now," Day said. "You couldn't know it but he's suspended and on Psych Review. Pending involuntary commitment."

"Royster, why didn't you tell me this?" Lenny barked.

Feeling like I was ten-years old and back in a kiddie sailor suit again, I just shrugged.

"That's no answer!" Anger made his raspy voice raspier.

"Maybe because you didn't ask me the question, 'Hey, Royster, are you headed for the home for the bewildered?'" I said. "Maybe I blocked it out. That's Freudian."

"Are these wisecracks worth your future?" Lenny asked.

"That depends," I said. "My future looks pretty dull without them."

"So you'll amuse yourself right into a Psych Review," Day said. "You're in love with your own destruction. I'm trying to supervise F. Scott Fitzgerald in a blue bag."

"Yay, Captain," I said. "City College lit professors will be happy that you remember old F. Scott."

"Lieutenant, you either arrest Royster now or let him slink home to his hole-in-the-wall," Day said. "I'm not standing still for an Illegal Detention charge in my precinct."

"You're joking, Captain."

"Try me."

"You just want to avoid one of your precinct cops getting arrested while you're in charge," Hundshamer said.

Both their voices were chopping out words faster.

Professionalism was shedding like snakeskin in the spring.

"You don't care about Royster," Lenny drove on. "You only care about your career."

Captain Day's Santa Claus head snapped up.

"How subtle you are," Day said. "No wonder that cuckoo cop ate your hand."

"Cuckoo cop did what?" I asked.

"Never mind."

"Sounds intriguing," I said. "What went down?"

"Nothing."

Lenny suddenly became a man of few words.

Other cops coming in and out of the precinct house stopped to watch our talk. There was never any privacy on the job.

They seemed to sense that Lenny was some kind of rat. Captain Day's face looked as if he were trying to eat a lemon without using his hands.

"Another sock salesman like you, who never should have gone on the Job, got caught running crack dealers or some such perversion," Day said. "Hundshamer of CRIT caught him dirty and handcuffed him. The cop went berserk and caught Hundshamer's hand in his mouth and tore it to hell. Like a bulldog. Nobody could get him stopped. No Taser or gas worked. Muscles, tendons and bones crunched up. Still hurts, Lieu?"

"Not anymore," he said.

"Cop got eight years for Maiming," Day said.

"Stop wasting time," he said. "I've got a homicide to clear. In your precinct."

"Then let my squad work it," Day said. "Or Manhattan North Homicide. Not CRIT. You aren't trained in homicide investigations."

"Just bad cops. And I think yours did this one."

"I don't care what you think," Day said. "Prove it and get enough for an arrest. Or else, good night."

My knees buckled a few inches.

"Thanks, Cap," I breathed out.

"Don't thank him," Lenny said. "He's only protecting his own pension."

"For whatever reason," I said. "I pay my bills."

"Pay it by going straight home," Day said. "Think about your options in life from now on."

"You mean fleeing the city," I said, "Losing the pension and getting a felony warrant on me anyway. And some country deputy in Nebraska will bust me anyway. That makes everything easier for the Job."

"And no lawsuit against the City," Lenny said.

"I can't tell Royster to flee," Day said. "That's against the law."

"Well, that would never do," I said. "Good night, gentlemen. I'm running home to pound my ear on my pillow."

"Step away from me, Royster," Lenny said, "and I'll lock you up."

That froze me.

Putting me through the system would mean two or three days in the Central Booking cage where madmen drooled and killers ruled. The papers would hear that I was a cop suspected of a sex killing and print my Academy photo.

It was time to run a bluff.

"On the charge of what, Lieu?" I asked.

"Murder."

"Oh, yeah," I winged it. "You got enough right now? Because I got an alibi that you will love."

Both supervisors looked at each other.

"What is it?" Lenny asked.

"Not now, Lieu," I said. "At trial. Which will never happen."

He stared at me. His mauled hand twitched. The torn nerves probably did it all the time.

"Get lost," he snapped.

For once, I obeyed.

CHAPTER 13.

Heading back to my apartment, I kept looking straight ahead.

Something felt like it was closing in on me. Surveillance is like true love. It's hard to describe. But you know when it is there.

In Mexico, cops from some internal security bureau used to watch me and follow me home. I never learned why. Maybe they had suspected me of remembering the Alamo. But they had kept it up long enough to fine-tune my eyes and nerves to being watched.

Tonight Hundshamer was probably doing it now. He was whistling up more team members, more CRITters, to help him tail me.

Well, I was going to make it easy for him. I was going to keep walking up Third Avenue, so he could stay in the uptown traffic behind me. He could leapfrog me in his car from block to block. I would not turn my head.

He could tail me to my door and put me to bed. He already had the address.

My building looked great. That meant that I was in real trouble because the sight of it usually depressed me. I was paying way too much rent to nest in this one-building slum.

ଓ

My body hit the futon and stretched out.

Sleep slipped away from me.

Maybe Day and Hundshamer bonded after I had left. They could combine forces. Day could get a tame police surgeon to sign papers calling me a psycho and drop me into Bellevue tonight. If I stayed put, they could use a warrant to get through my front door.

"No good," I said. "That would put our hero in sorrow's clutch."

No matter how silly patrolling 83rd Street might be, it was better than trying to crack the killing from inside a Bellevue cell.

So I switched on every light in the apartment and fashioned a dummy in my bed. By morning, they might have someone with binoculars on a nearby roof. If they thought that I was in bed, it might buy me time.

I had no TV. My FM radio set switched on. Anyone listening might think that I was still at home.

"Uh, oh," I said aloud.

Headlights swept the street outside my apartment. A woman that I had never seen before slipped from the car. Her black poncho only made her chunky figure chunkier. Blue jeans and sneakers showed below.

She went out of my view for a second, then sat on a stoop up the block and took out cigarettes. She lit one.

I waited.

The same car came around my block again.

She nodded to the car.

That was Hundshamer's CRITters team. If they were as subtly dressed as this woman, then I was in big trouble. They could tail me invisibly tomorrow and I would never see the others.

I was lucky to spot this woman now. They were playing it for a tight tail now. So I had the advantage on an empty street. But it would not last.

Scooping all my spare cash into my pockets, I left my apartment and tiptoed up towards the roof.

ಌ

Everything seemed to scream "MADMAN! STOP!"

My breath racked in and out.

The stairs creaked.

I kept going higher.

The roof door opened under my super's gift key.

I stepped out onto the room, smelling hot tar and stale beer from the afternoon.

The next building's roof was about nine feet away and lower than mine.

But heights often froze me. Talking down suicide jumpers was a job that I had gladly given to Emergency Services. I had no stomach for it.

"Only nine feet," I said. "No problem."

But my voice betrayed me.

"Don't look down," I whispered. "That way, everything is fine."

With a running start, I jumped.

I looked down.

"Everything is un-fine," I said.

A world of concrete opened beneath me.

The gap between the buildings yawned.

It seemed to grow.

My arms flailed.

It felt like I was not going anyway.

My foot hit the roof parapet.

The ankle twisted.

I landed on top of it.

The whole old body flopped down onto the other roof.

"Un-fine," I kept chanting.

Rolling across the tarry roof, clutching my ankle, I felt the pain corkscrew and seem to take off the top of my head.

"But alive," I said.

Bracing myself on the roof-top shed, I could stand and walk a few steps with my left ankle throbbing.

"Not good enough for ComPol," I told myself. "The neighbors on 83rd Street will be bringing me a cane. The surveillance team will be looking at my building. This building's door opens onto the next street. Now let our hero limp into the night and sleep at Leo's garage. If he can get there."

CHAPTER 14.

Someone was barking questions at me.

I woke up on the floor Leo's garage. Everything in me ached.

"What you doing here, bro'?"

Something clanged near my ear.

"Talking to you, man. What's up, player?"

My left eye opened.

"Leo knows me," I said. "Everything's okay."

The fewer facts, the better, I figured.

"Yeah? I'm Leo's supervisor –"

"Oh, that word," I whispered.

"– and he's not running no youth hostel for bums like you here. Hit the bricks, homeboy."

A mullet hair-do over a tight-lipped face bobbed before my bleary eyes. My contact lenses were out for sleeping, so I squinted at him, blurry in the garage cot room.

He looked like a quarrelsome forty-something, young to me, and happy to lay down the law. Muscles bulged against the orange T-shirt and blue jeans that he wore.

A meaningless tattoo scored his thick left forearm. My forearms never looked like that, no matter how much I twisted elastic bands and pumped out scores of midnight push-ups.

"I'll ask Leo why he's letting you flop here," the Supervisor said. "And why he needs a spare locker all of a sudden. Is your stuff in the locker? We can't be legally responsible."

"No, sir. I've got a diabetic condition and was about to collapse last night. Leo did not know that I was coming here."

Air-headed women would call him good-looking. His face twisted.

"You drop dead here and we can't be responsible," he said. "You could sue us."

"From the grave?"

"Says which?"

"Nothing, sir," I said. "I'm leaving now. Thank you for your consideration."

"Yeah, yeah. Come back and I feed you to the cops."

East 87th Street looked like a commercial entitled "Move to Arizona Today."

Gray, oily clouds colored the sky and wet street underneath it. Someone's pizza dinner wafted up from the trash can nearby. Wetness from a puddle came through my Reebok soles. My socks were sodden.

"Fantastic," I groused. "Just what I need."

My watch said 6:17.

"Our hero needs a place to flop down hard," I said.

I started cellphoning friends.

They fed me their voicemail.

Or else they ignored the phone.

Raindrops started flecking downwards.

My socks took on more water.

Jody was a teacher at Hunter College, I recalled. That would make her a city worker, like me.

So I called the Municipal Credit Union 24-hour customer service line.

"MCU, how can I help you?" a bored Queensy accent said.

"My aunt," I said, slurring my words into some kind of accent. Spanish, I hoped. "She get her purse lost when the police car hit her brother-in-law's Raymundo's gypsy cab that he had not finished with the payments –"

The clerk blew out breath.

I did not blame her.

"MCU," she repeated. "How can I help you?"

Rattling her would work. I needed her rattled and short-term angry, panting to tell her co-workers about this moron calling her at this time of the night. Or else, my hustle would not work.

"She cannot find her bankbook, and she just moved and does not remember, 'cause it was somewhere else. And I don't know… Her name is Jody… and she going to want me to cancel the credit cards –"

"What's her last name, sir?"

"*Desculpe*?"

"Sir, I don't speak Spanish."

"I sorry, sorry. Excuse me extremely. Her last name, that's Quinanna."

"And where does she live?"

"That's what I try tell you. She just move from that place."

"I've got a Jody Quirianna at 41 Hamilton Terrace in Manhattan."

Got it! I told myself.

"That's not it," I said. "Not 'Quirianna.' I didn't tell you 'Quirianna.'"

"Sir, you were mumbling very badly."

"She say it different, ma'am. Let me call you back."

She hung up.

I sagged against the booth.

"I don't blame her," I said. "She may need a shot to get through the rest of the day."

41 Hamilton Terrace, here we come.

ঙ

Morning sounds clicked around me. Birds cheeped in the scrabby trees on this Harlem side street.

41 Hamilton Place boasted brownstone walls and an outside staircase, with tasteful black shuttered windows. Other brownstones crowded the block. There was just an occasional horn toot from Amsterdam Avenue. Broom bristles rasped the sidewalks as residents washed them down and looked at me.

A bouquet of daisies moved in my left hand. With the other one, I held a cotton duffle bag, bulging at the bottom.

Jody would not be really happy to see me at seven something on a rainy wet morning. We had parted crudely at the murder scene. This called for fashioning something attractive for her.

I cracked open my jaw and sang:

> "O Shenan-do-ah!
> I'm going to leave you!
> Roll away, you rolling river!"

"What's all that truck outside?" a sleepy voice rumbled from an open window to my left.

It made me grin. My singing was rupturing local real estate values.

"Some white man singing."

Nobody was applauding But faint heart never won fair maiden.

This had been an all-black neighborhood before. Now white faces mixed with black faces in the generously-built windows. Harlem's elite had lived in this neighborhood. The architecture showed the ornate turns of the wealthy.

These were families where nobody had changed their own car tires in a century.

The brownstones spoke of a past era of jitterbuggers, Harlem dandies in three-piece suits with watch-chains and pomaded moustaches. Some private garages sloped down under the brownstones.

"I'm calling the po-po!" someone else shouted. "Police can handle a crazy person like this one."

"Why don't you ignore all this?" another neighbor said. "Just enjoy the music."

"That's an old song."

"What next? There goes the neighborhood."

Hearing that old cliché about the neighborhood made me grin.

A blue-and-white NYPD car sashayed from the corner towards me.

This was trouble that I did not need. Lenny may have put a warrant out on me already. These two might put the arm on me and wedge me into the back seat.

The Driver Officer, a chunky Asian with gold Cazale glasses that hinted at his vanity, peered at me through the rain.

My legs shook.

Things were getting worser.

His partner, the Recorder Officer, slouched back in her seat. Her heavy black hair, cut short, touched her uniform collar. She looked like someone who had their time in and wanted to retire. I knew the look, even from far away. She dandled an iced coffee in her wide hands. That might save me. Most cops did not want to waste time policing when they had invested in a drink.

I kept singing.

Their windows hung three inches open, in good patrol style.

They seemed to squint right down my throat.

The car nosed towards me.

I started walking away from my spot.

They could ignore whatever they saw.

My feet kept walking.

"Hey, Romeo!" the Recorder cop said over the Public Address system in the car. The noise echoed on Hamilton Place. "Don't stop now. You're going strong."

This was her way of slamming the ones living on Hamilton Place. Most cops hated working Harlem, for the dangers and the hatred that tailed them everywhere.

She would never act this way in the Playpen.

The blue-and-white passed me and kept going.

I stopped walking and picked up the song again.

"Why are you doing this?" a young girl's voice asked.

I kept on belting out the song.

> "O Shen-an-do-ah!
> I love your daught-er!
> Roll away,
> You rolling riv-ver!"

Rain sounds started. Drops hissed on the heating sidewalks.

Rain was dropping down on me and my flowers. Another drop touched onto my head.

More windows opened up along Hamilton Place. I tucked my chin down and tried pitching my voice lower. Fewer disasters happened that way.

Inside 41, a light came on. A blonde teenager peered outside and then ducked her head back inside.

From my distance, she had Jody's hair and looks.

She came back outside, seemed to giggle and then went back inside.

My songs kept churning on.

So did the rain.

Another head leaned out of 41.

This was Jody herself, dressed in a scarlet bathrobe.

"Get away from here," she said.

"Now, what do we mean by that?" I said. "Yeah, what do we mean by that?"

"Leave me and my family alone."

She was about twenty feet in front of me.

Smiling as the rainwater coursed down my cheeks, I tried approaching her.

She started to draw back inside.

"I need some help," I said.

"That seems plain."

I let her have that one.

"Mature people don't do things like this," she said. "Go away or I'll call your buddies on the police."

"I don't have any."

"I'll call."

"I think that serenading is protected under the First Amendment. Freedom of Speech and that pursuit of happiness mess. But I need your help in my 'copera'."

"What is a 'copera?'" Jody asked.

"Well. You know what a cop is, right?"

"I used to think so," she said.

"Well, put the two words 'cop' and 'opera' together. A cop who performs in an opera, like today, is putting forth a copera. It blends the two art forms."

A neighbor leaned down from her window.

"Take him in!" the neighbor shouted. She was a scattered-looking white woman about 60, sporting a New York Yankees baseball hat against the rain. "Can't you see that he's getting wet? What kind of girlfriend are you?"

"Good question," I said.

"How long are you going to stalk me like this?" Jody asked.

"You see now how important the police are to a well-ordered society."

The same blonde teenage girl that I had seen before bobbed up in the doorway behind Jody.

"Jody, you'd do better taking him inside and end the show," she said. "This way he's just getting more attention."

"That's what psychopaths crave," Jody said. "Come here, Max. But just until the crowd loses interest."

I came towards the brownstone door, now speckled with rain.

Some neighbors clapped. Some others cat-called.

"Cameo, this is Mister Royster," Jody said. "Please don't talk to him. He's a tempting waste of time."

"Jody talked about you already," Cameo said. She stood an inch or so taller than Jody's five-seven. The same glossy blonde hair fell to her wide strong shoulders. The women in this family seemed built for outdoor work. Both Jody and her daughter would have looked comfortable cutting brush in the wilderness.

Jody's determined look had not come down to Cameo yet. The pigtails said that she was not taking herself too seriously yet. The high cheekbones and pouty mouth made her look like a rah-rah party girl at a beach barbecue.

"Max, Cameo is getting to work in a little while," Jody said. "So just say hello and goodbye. It's unlikely you'll see each other again."

"In the highest tradition of copera," I said, "the show must go on."

"What's a 'copera?'" Cameo asked.

"Don't ask," Jody said. "Don't encourage him."

We were entering the kitchen of the three-story brownstone. The walls and furniture lacked decoration. Jody had probably put her life's savings into buying the house. City College did not pay their teachers a treasure in salary.

"How did you get my address?" Jody asked.

"Dostoevsky says that we need more mysteries in life," I said.

"It's maddening how you keep wisecracking. You think that everything is a joke."

The walls were a dark reddish clay color. A brick fire place showed that the builder worried about cold winter nights. Ashes and wood chunks lay inside the fireplace. Jody believed in using whatever the brownstone offered.

Books flowed everywhere, in streams of brown or black leather. Someone liked collecting leather editions. The books lay on shelves and tables. Titles from Hume, Kant, Aquinas and Schopenhauer winked at me in gold lettering.

"Erudite stuff here, Professor," I said, nodding at the books.

"Some of them are Cam's," Jody said.

"Which ones?"

"The ones that I can't keep up with."

"Does this mean that you know a lot about philosophy?" I asked.

"I know enough to avoid trouble that I can't handle," she said. "You seem to fall into that category."

I made a hushing motion with my hand and pointed at Cameo. Jody's face flushed under her antique gold hair.

"Follow me to the living room," Jody said. "Where you will sleep until I go out for my class. There are pillows on the sofa. Or the floor, if you feel like it."

"I'm not as manly as all that," I said.

"No?"

"No," I said. "I'm the toughest guy in my ballet class."

She brought me to the second floor and opened the door to a small living room with tables, a wide-screen TV in the corner and the promised sofa. An old leather chair gave off a scent in the air turned humid.

"Rain's getting stronger outside," I said. "It's another Manhattan storm in summer, fierce and unpredictable."

Drops hammered the old windows.

"Good sleeping weather," Jody said. She moved to the door and closed it behind her.

I made a hump of comfy pillows and put my head down.

My body unkinked and spread over the hardwood floor. The head lolled. I had the feeling of reaching, reaching, far back behind me.

That was the last thing that I remembered.

☙

The door clicked open.

Jody came inside, dressed for teaching now, in a charcoal-colored shirtwaist.

"We have to be out the front door in ten minutes," she said.

"Then this is probably the wrong time to ask for my own key."

"Do you know why I let you in this morning?"

"Curiosity."

"Because I need to get that sabbatical job teaching in Italy," she said. "It's vital for Cameo and me. It will give me breathing room from some debts here. My accountant keeps reminding me that I could lose this house."

"How?"

"Some clause in my mortgage," Jody said. "Penalty. Something too complex for me to grasp, Try as I may. But it's real. And Italy can stop this from happening."

"You could always stow me away and smuggle me into Italy. Italy likes serenading. They started it."

"But before I can be accepted for this post overseas, City College hires an outside firm to conduct a background check on me. Finances, credit and what neighbors say about me."

"That's exactly the kind of Big Brother stuff that City College screams about us cops doing," I said.

"Nevertheless, they are doing one on me."

"That means that, when it comes to cash, City College is just like the rest of us," I said.

"Neighbors may report that drunken men come and go singing near my building. That does not help me get overseas."

"Not unless you're going to Ireland."

"So you started off today by imperiling my career –"

"Let us imperil this," I said.

I stepped closer and kissed her. Today she smelled of a coconut scent.

Her muscles tensed against me. My fingertips could feel the steel of her body.

"Don't do this!" she hissed, breaking away.

I stepped back.

"Of course not," I said. "Whatever was I thinking of?"

"That's what I would like to know."

"There will be students waiting for their teacher to show up on time for class. We have to leave now."

The living room and the comfy pillows that had sheltered me seemed very small now.

"I keep seeing that you're in a male detective fantasy," she said. "The responsible thing for you to do is surrender to the courts."

"Then who will hunt this Horn Bug? Your Philosophy Department?"

"Not you."

We scrutinized each other.

"There's a lawyer that I know named Felix," she said. "She's brilliant and dynamic and my close friend. Go back to your superiors, and I'll ask her to defend you *pro bono*. She won't charge you."

"She sounds like an unusual barrister."

"She already defends strangers for free. I know she'll commit to you."

"Don't use that word 'commit,' please," I said.

"But I know people like you always delay. So my offer ends this Friday. If you haven't matured by then, you probably won't. But I guarantee that Felix can get the supervisors in your department to leave you alone."

We stepped back down the staircase. I wondered briefly about Jody's bedroom upstairs and what it looked like. My thoughts drifted to how it might feel waking up with her there.

"You're going to a lot of trouble for me," I said.

"Really? I'm protecting myself, Max. I look at you and see a lot worse trouble up ahead."

CHAPTER 15.

Body shaking and trying to rest, I called Jody from Leo's garage that afternoon.

"Our hero will need something heavier than a left jab if he ever finds this Horn Bug," I told Jody over the phone that afternoon.

"You seem to think that you're one of the Hardy Boys," she said. "And that I want to play Nancy Drew with you. Giving you my cell number was as far as it goes. You're on your own."

"Please don't hang up."

She hung up.

The garage smelled of oil slicks and Leo's thick cigars.

"That teaching job in Italy has turned her head," I said. "How could she fail to love our hero?"

Leo smirked when he saw my face. He had the sidekick's knack of sensing moods.

"*Gna Oy Nay,*" he said.

"He always says that when he sees you," a slim blonde woman said. She waited for her husband in the garage each afternoon at the same time. "What does it mean?"

"I used to work in Hong Kong," I said. "Picked up some Cantonese. Leo heard me talk it once and wanted to know how to say 'I love you' in Cantonese. So I taught him the phrase. '*Gna Oy Nay.*"

"Now it's his mantra," she said.

"That's why Max stop the bums from come around, break into cars and say they gonna cut me," Leo said. "He use the big words on them, and they scared."

"Well," she said. "My hero."

"No," Leo said. "My hero."

I removed a green Army duffle bag from my uniform locker and emptied the spare uniform and gunbelt on the floor. I slung it half-filled over my shoulder for an afternoon of speed shopping.

Someone was playing classical piano behind the garage. Notes floated over the cracked concrete.

The woman driver kept looking at Leo. Maybe she wondered why he seemed so happy.

Reaching back to my Academy days, I called a few classmates from there. I asked them to loan me any kind of gun.

"Anything light that you picked up," I kept saying. "Nothing pricey. Or with a bad story stuck with it."

They refused. Some sounded scared.

"Any gun that you found," I said. "Nothing traceable."

"Royster, I can't believe that you're this desperate," one said. "You're really reaching."

Then I called Lipkin and asked him.

"Why you calling me?" he asked.

"Because you're Ireland's last hope," I said.

"Me loan you a piece?" Lipkin asked. "You are deluded. Still a Funny Bunny."

"Come on, Al."

"You keep boring me with how much you hate guns."

"After what I have seen them do, yes. But I need a throwaway piece now."

"The city has maybe two gunshops left. And they won't sell to you without papers. You got those papers? Scuttlebutt has it that the DA is ready to indict you for Elspeth's murder."

"Which I didn't do, Al. But I need a gun."

"Why don't you ask Hundshamer?"

"Cop gossip wins again."

"Wisecracks won't keep you from Bellevue. Max, maybe you should ask yourself why you are always the petitioner. Always asking everybody to risk ruin for you. That can't be an accident."

CHAPTER 16.

Gun laws had some loopholes.

I planned to crash through them.

I took a subway and bus odyssey to Brighton Beach in Brooklyn, where thousands of Russian refugees had fled to create new lives.

I bought a *Post* at a newsstand, then dropped some more money in a large hardware store where the clerks chattered to each other in Russian.

I called Rhea, a civil lawyer that I knew from ballroom dancing at Sessions 73. We chatted about law. She said that she would be in her office all evening.

Flea markets bloomed in the narrow streets near the beach. Acres of aging furniture, Eastern Orthodox icons and leather-bound volumes with titles in the Cyrillic alphabet.

"What you looking for?" the hawkers kept asking me in chalk-and-honey accents.

I scrabbled through a table where a skeletal man, shaved head and red eye patch, was calling out "Tools! Metal tools!"

The table looked a weary century old, of carved mahogany, with brass drawers.

I kept digging through piles of metal and tin. Rust flaked off and gathered in my finger crevices. Something smelled like rotting meat.

Heat grew in this basement. The empty duffle bag kept sliding off my shoulder.

It smelled of old uniforms.

"Nothing here," I said. "I'll keep looking. Thanks."

I struggled through one basement and into another.

I pawed through another yard of everything.

After hours of discouragement, I bobbed to the surface.

"I told you that I'm making on an indie film," I told the Headman who stared over his yards of riches.

"So, what you need?"

"Just this," I said.

What I lifted out of the pile of tools, saws and car fenders was a long, double-barreled goose gun with rusted hammers. The shotgun had some sort of filigreed shield etched into the breech and a variety of cryptic markings stamped into the base of the barrel. The crafted balance kept it lightly in my hand.

"I cannot sell to you." The Headman was a hawk-faced slim athlete with salt-and-pepper hair and a face darkened by five o'clock shadow. If people were animals, he would be a peppy greyhound, always snapping.

That chagrined our hero.

"You must have a long gun, shotgun or rifle, license," he said in the choppy accent. "If you have, show to me."

It was time to challenge the conventional wisdom again.

"Not for this fine old antique," I said. "Check your sales record. I'll bet you a wedding breakfast that this gun was made before 1899."

"So?"

"So, legally speaking, that makes it an antique. Not capable of being fired. No license needed. Look."

I showed him a Xerox sheet from the Webster Branch of the Public Library on York and 78th Street.

"'No license or other permit shall be required,'" I read to him.

"I could go to jail!"

"Not for this. Something else, probably."

"Let me call boss."

"When you finish with the Bossa Nova, call this lawyer," I said, palming him Rhea's business card. The cardboard had wilted from months in my wallet. "She will tell you the same."

"Why you need this gun?"

"Oh, the suspicious mind. We're putting on a play."

"You said 'a movie.'"

"Play first, then movie."

"What play, please?"

"*Kleptomaniac Sex-Monsters from the Tanning Salon*. It's a Sundance shoo-in."

"I don't know."

"Make your calls. Call the police, if you want to."

He barked into the phone at someone named Svetlana and then an Andrei for some time. He scrutinized me and then sounded as if he were describing me. The description did not take long.

"Sex," he said to me.

"What about it?"

"Sex."

"That old thing?"

"Sex hundred dollars, why you make jokes? Buy this!"

"For six hundred dollars? Does it work?"

"Do I need to know this?" he asked. "Is antique. My boss says to sell."

"You are right, my friend," I said. Hundred dollar bills fanned out from my pocket. My fingers hated to see them go.

He handed me the gun.

I hefted it again.

My scheme looked silly now but the money was already spent.

It took some wheedling but the dealer swathed the gun in brown wrapping paper. He tore his signature across the scrap of paper that served as a receipt.

The goose gun fit into the duffle bag.

I hoisted it.

The barrel stuck out.

I ripped today's *Post* and ruffled the pages around the barrel. Scotch tape did the rest. The newspaper covering the barrel looked weird, but not like it was concealing a shotgun.

"Where do you go with this thing?" he asked.

"Out of your store forever, good sir," I said.

"And what you do with it?"

"Just a prop in my upcoming film. Watch for it on the Sundance Channel."

CHAPTER 17.

"Two boxes of that double-ought buck, please," I said.

"May I see your shotgun permit, sir?" The clerk looked like a black-bearded pirate, with long hair gathered in a braid and fierce light-colored eyes. Power-lifter muscles bunched under his Hawaiian surfer shirt.

I tucked my chin lower, a habit from boxing.

"For what?" I asked. "I'm only buying ammunition. And for a long gun."

"That's our store policy, sir," he said.

Breath whistled out of my nose.

"What about our state law?" I asked.

"Store policy, sir."

"You keep saying that. What about my right to buy ammunition to save myself ? I'm in a terribly carnivorous neighborhood. And I don't want to be eaten up."

"Our store goes with the spirit of the law, sir. We have our own system of checks and balances. I'm sure that you don't want the wrong people firing guns."

"What are you doing working in a gun store?" I asked. "You're as misplaced as I am."

It took three more stores but I scored three boxes of 12 gauge shotgun ammunition into my duffle bag.

☙

I journeyed back to Manhattan. Now I needed to make sure that my shotgun worked. Shooting it off anywhere might bring the cops. So I needed a remote place.

The FDR Drive along the East River.

I got onto the pedestrian walkway at 96th Street, near the white-framed square of Gracie Mansion, home of the mayor. He would probably become somewhat nettled if I tested my new toy in his backyard.

"Crazed Ex-Cop in Assassination Attempt!" the tabloids would scream.

Instead, I footed the path up to a footbridge on east 103rd Street and crossed over the river to Ward's Island.

Most New Yorkers never walked the 255 greenish acres and river walks of Ward's Island. Some avoided it because Bellevue Hospital had sent their criminally insane patients to the Kirby Center on the island. Patients sometimes roamed the island on daily passes. Kirby Center smothered any news of attacks or escapes.

They did not want the public alarmed.

Sometimes Kirby would notify the Job that some patient who had been showing great promise had apparently cut loose and was taking a foot tour somewhere in the city. They would fax us faded photocopies and ask that the patient be counseled and returned.

But the island boasted river views and quiet glades of sunny greenery. Bold souls enjoyed treading and biking here.

Finding an isolated spot near the river, I checked to make sure that nobody was slumbering nearby. The pathway looked empty.

Tugboats churned past on the river. I found the thickest grove of trees so that nobody could see me from the river. The Job and the U.S. Coast Guard patrolled the river, hunting for any signs of terrorists.

If they saw me, they might whistle up a blue-and-white to sniff me out.

So I sat and waited for dark, thinking about my future.

When full dark came, I slipped my wrapped shotgun out of the duffle, thinking of what name I might dub it. 'Hopeless' formed the strongest choice.

"Orville, I doubt that it will fly," I said aloud.

Talking to myself would land me in Bellevue. Then Bellevue would ship me here, to Kirby.

Desecrating an antique, I played the hacksaw against the wooden stock and started sawing. The noise rasped but would not carry far.

My arm worked the saw.

I was slicing the stock off by the pistol grip just to the rear of the trigger. The stock had to be short. Shooting a shotgun without one would blast it back into your arm and rock you with its recoil. But the buckshot will spread and destroy anyone in front of you. I needed to see how my blast pattern would work with this shotgun.

The stock dropped off.

Then I sawed the double barrels down.

They clunked down onto the ground.

Now the whole gun was sawn down to about eleven inches, six of it the twin barrels.

"Just holding this little baby will win me seven years in prison," I said. "That's because lawmakers saw how deadly the blast is. It is worse than any assault rifle."

Ignoring ecology, I dropped both the stock and cut barrels into the blue-black waters.

"No evidence for trial, in case I get grabbed up," I thought. "They could raise fingerprints from what was left."

Using a handful of stones, I fitted the shotgun into a kind of vise and pointed it downwards into the river. Shooting it might dislodge it from the stones but not by much. Then I took off my left shoelace and tied it to the twin triggers. I fastened the shoelace to my belt and took off my belt.

I tore off pieces from *The Post,* wetted them in my mouth and wedged them into my ears.

"Perfect use for *The Post*," I said aloud. "It was the only paper available today. New York's kindergarten newspaper."

The barrels looked clear, but I had to test everything.

I lay flat on the ground to the left of the vise-gripped shotgun.

"Any explosion should go over my head," I muttered. 'That's some scrap from memory of tenth-grade physics."

The river waters coursed past.

If any shrapnel hit my eyes, this might the last thing that I saw.

Praying to my household gods, I drew on the string gently, to gauge the trigger pull.

The shoelace tensed.

A roar blasted my ears.

The shotgun leaped backwards from the vise.

A shock wave blasted the hair on my moustache and my pants legs flapped backwards.

It felt like someone had clapped their hands over my ears.

I flattened some more, waiting to recover.

My ears rang and hummed.

"Well, the little wonder works," I said aloud. That tested my hearing. My voice sounded far away, as if some cotton was blocking my ears. When I swallowed, the noise of my throat working seemed to stay inside my head.

Moving swiftly in case anyone heard, I went back to the shotgun.

Recoil had driven the shotgun a foot back from my homemade vise.

I broke the shotgun open and put two more red shells into the barrels. It snapped shut.

I replaced my shoelace and threaded the belt back on.

Worried about evidence again, I heaved the stones into the river.

Then I walked down to the water's edge. If I fired at a tree to see the blast pattern, the trunk might blast some of the buckshot back at me. Explaining that wound to an ER might be dicey. They would feed me to the Job.

But I needed to see how the buckshot spread.

Wrapping both hands around the shotgun stump, I tucked it in tightly against my gut, away from the ribcage and picked out a spot on the water.

Then I slowly squeezed the trigger.

The shotgun bucked against my gut.

Barrels tipped upwards.

The same roar batted at my ears.

The buckshot worked.

A three- or four-foot patch of water spurted up out of the river.

"There's the shot pattern," I said. "From ten feet away, anything in front of these barrels turns to pudding."

I hoped that I would not have to use it.

Listening, I stayed where I was.

The island seemed still. Nobody reacted to the blasts.

I broke open the shotgun and tossed the shells into the river.

Then I walked back to where the duffle bag lay.

A breeze riffled along the river.

Bird noises sounded in the night.

Carrying a loaded shotgun was too much of a risk. Nobody had run a safety test on it during this century. It might go off at any time. Metal parts could rust or just give up the ghost to metal fatigue.

Or someone from the Job might stop me. Carrying it loaded meant a lot more prison upstate.

So it stayed broken in the duffle bag.

I shouldered the duffle bag and started moving through the darkened trees to the concrete footpath. The smell of trees and dirt released themselves after a hot afternoon.

☙

"Shooting is bad," a man's voice said. "We see you shooting."

I jumped backwards and stopped dead.

"Why do you mess our nice island with shooting?"

A blocky figure of a man showed in the park's lamplight. He stood a head taller than I did. Silver hair cut in bangs showed above his pale face that the sun never touched.

"Not your business, brother man," I said. "It's been a longish day, you know? I don't want a war with anyone. So just let me pass."

"Maybe he thinks that you're alone, Jeffcoat," a woman's voice said behind me.

That made me spin around.

A slim-shaped woman with blonde hair gleaming in the half-light leaned near me with a stick aimed at my groin. The stick held a sharp spear point, smeared with something. It smelled like dog dung.

I bit my lower lip.

A line of other figures encircled me.

The half-light showed some holding sticks and rocks.

"We gotta travel in packs, like this, grouped up to protect our own asses, check it out," she said. "Whenever anyone screws with us."

"I'm not screwing with you," I said.

"Oh, yeah," the man named Jeffcoat sneered. "You're the cuckoo bird, with your big gun shooting up our home."

They ranged from their 20s to some who looked to be aging past 60. They all wore washed-out hospital greens.

One snickered.

Another spat and caught me across the face with his spit.

Talking seemed important.

"I'm no threat," I said.

"We don't know about that," Jeffcoat, the big pale shape in front of me said. "You seem quite dangerous to us with that noisy gun of yours."

"You square suckers call us 'crazy.' But you don't see those attendant stealing our watches or messing up our heads to fight each other. So they can bet on us. Like dogs."

"And you free-worlders come here sometimes and light us up with gas fires," Jeffcoat rasped. "Makes you wonder who is really crazy."

"Not for long," a woman croaked.

"That's a flipping question that goddamn well answers itself."

"And we have no rights and no press," the woman behind me said.

"Carla, some staff care," Jeffcoat said.

"Hah!" Carla said. She stepped closer. Now I could see her light blonde hair tumbled over a sculpted athlete's face. The muscles worked as she screwed up her face. She looked about thirty. Her voice came softly out from a sensual mouth made for smiling and kissing. "I did all that family counseling long enough to see apathy set in. Then the work finally got to me. Me, who everyone trusted with their secrets."

My legs tensed, wanting to flee without hurting anyone here.

"Carla, you're wasting time," Jeffcoat said.

"And I feel the attendants' hands roughing me up in my secret skin," Carla said. "Scavengers like this one come to our island to rape any lady patient that they can find. Who is going to believe us?"

"Too much talk," Jeffcoat said.

He rushed me.

"Awwww!" I keened.

Fear dumbed me down.

I skittered backwards, flinging the duffle bag at him.

The shotgun inside flew against his head.

It stopped him.

Nancy's lesson came back to me.

I side-stepped Jeffcoat's bull rush.

My left leg came up in an angle kick against his thigh. I turned my hip into it. The foot hit. He stopped and slipped down.

With my foot, I stomped his shin against the ground.

He tried seizing me but I dodged.

He grabbed his foot and rolled away, cussing.

Carla advanced.

The stick she brandished had a long kitchen knife tied with twine at the end. She could stick me with it like a bayonet before I reached her.

Another woman alongside her waved an old-fashioned straight razor.

"Look, I don't want to hurt anyone here," I said.

"Don't worry about that," Carla said. "We'll hurt you too, first."

"I could be sharing showers with you next week," I said.

"What a cleesh!"

"You mean 'cliché,'' another one corrected.

"I feel that we are not so different," I said.

"We've heard that before," Carla said. "Prove it."

To convince them, I talked about myself, the Job and Day's threat to psycho me in ten days. Nerves made my voice climb higher.

A tugboat went by on the river.

I thought about jumping in and swimming for Manhattan. But I would lose the shotgun that I needed so badly.

Some of them cussed. A few rocked on the ground.

Shadows moved away into the trees.

Some shadows bent over Jeffcoat. They ministered to him, the only softness that he would know.

My breath hawked down deep in my body.

"I hate hurting people," I said. "Sorry, Mister Jeffcoat."

Most kept me encircled, walking me backwards until I slipped onto the footbridge, feeling my legs shake with every step and feeling their eyes slither over me.

CHAPTER 18.

The next morning, I farmed the sidewalk on East 83rd again, back in sunlight and in my copera. My body felt relieved.

"Good morning," I said to a man scrubbing a stoop.

Small and delicately built, he crouched over the brownstone step. His dark eyes glinted, holding secrets. An unlit cheroot bobbed in his mouth.

"Nice day, beatnik," I said from inside my uniform, fixing my fake gunbelt and looking for something to say. "Good job that you're doing on that stoop."

The man did not answer. He kept slopping water and suds on the steps.

"I'm kind of new on the beat and wondered if I could do anything, make it better for you."

"Three-thirty, the kids come from Wagner and hang on the corner," he said in some kind of Slavic accent. "Make all kinds noise. Cutting the fool. You come stop them."

More ComPol cowflop, I told myself.

"Three-thirty?" I said. "Sure."

"One little asshole, they call Bo, always blocking the sidewalk. You give him a ticket for that, right? Call his parents and tell them, 'Come to station and pick him up'."

"Sure," I said.

If he thought that I could do that, he needed Bellevue, not me.

"Call all their families," he said. "They don't live here. Uptown trash, making trouble every day. Come back and break things."

My left leg dragged a bit. The sawed-off shotgun rode under the blue pants-leg, along my calf. A strong rubber-and-Velcro wrap from Falk Surgery on East 64th Street held it fast to my flesh. The NYPD uniform hung baggy on me so there was no bulge.

With practice, I could stoop down, lift the pants leg and draw the shotgun.

Teenage gangsters carried shotguns like this. They called themselves 'capmen.'

Eddie the beer-drinker crossed the street, saw me and kept going.

"Hello, Eddie," I called out. "Nice to see you."

A woman, hair the same flame color as mine, leaned her curved cello of a body out of a ground floor window, her wild eyes playing tricks.

"Hey, good-looking, what you got cooking?" she asked me.

She smiled like the Cheshire Cat.

A missing front tooth showed some trouble. Maybe her man beat her sometimes. It happened everywhere. It kept me wanting to work as a cop.

"Good evening, my dear," I said.

Her smile said that she knew a lot about us cops.

"You're making sure that I'm safe?" she asked. "Here in apartment 3-C, I mean."

"You look very safe to me," I lied.

"I do?"

It was time to give an avuncular grunt and keep walking. The patrol officer should always stay neutral.

But I kept my hips and gunbelt and toy gun turned to her. Pounding this beat was growing draggy. The Horn Bug might be summering in Lapland by now.

This temptress in the window promised adventure.

"Please come around just to make sure," she said.

It was time some snappy talk to answer her.

"I do that for everyone," I said.

She just kept smiling.

Some women chased cops looking for father figures. Or else they suffered psychological demons. We police wordsmiths called them "Badge Bunnies."

If a Funny Bunny mated with a Badge Bunny, would their offspring be Funny Badges?

My ankle kept aching.

The same kind of women who liked soldier-types would like the Horn Bug. She might know him. I would need to speak with her.

☙

Another stop was a tiny Korean grocery that smelled of doggy fluids. The slim bouncy owner at the register kept pressing a free soda on me and saying that everything was great.

"Okay, okay," he repeated. "No problem, officer."

"Yessir, beatnik," I said. "I know that the cops in Korea are bullies. Got no ComPol concept over there."

He just kept the talk rolling.

Years of dealing with cops had taught him how to survive.

"Yeah, there's something for you to do," a fat woman on the stoop said. "That red Jap car always parks right in front here. It's got commercial plates so it doesn't get a ticket. But that's phony. Can you put a note asking them what their business is, and why don't they park on First Avenue?"

This was why cops yearned to leave Patrol behind and get into a desk detail somewhere.

"You see that pothole there?" a freckle-faced dog walker in his fifties said, pointing a menthol cigarette at a two-foot pothole on the street, west of First Avenue.

"Absolutely," I said.

"Months, I've been calling the city to have it filled in. DOT, Department of Transportation. Assemblyman Dreifast, local blockwatchers, 311 hotline, different jerks on city payroll. We are like everyone else on this block. We see problems and crimes. And we see cops. And we wonder why cops do not seem to care about fixing those problems."

ComPol high priests would love this guy.

"I'll look into that," I said. I unfolded the sketch of the Horn Bug. "Have you ever seen this chap anywhere?"

He ticked his head down and up.

"No. Never. Is this something important?"

"He may have raped and murdered a woman in this neighborhood recently."

"Yeah," he said. "Now what can you do about this gitta-mort pothole?"

The word 'gitta-mort' sounded horrid but I did not know what it meant.

"As soon as I can," I said.

Manhattan always seemed like a moving sidewalk, moving way too fast for me.

Rapid talk, faster drinking, with professionals clipping their talk short so that everyone would know how important they were.

But East 83rd Street sometimes felt like a dreamy backwater. The pace slowed here. Not everybody was mad-dashing to the Iron Horse, the IRT station on 86th Street and Lexington. Candy shops, drycleaners, groceries and fortune tellers held small spots for the past forty years, trying to avoid the skyrocketing rents. And they hung on.

Beatniks sat smoking on stoops and greeted each other. I gladhanded all the ones that I saw. They nodded at the word 'beatnik.'

Some ignored me. Safe neighborhoods like this one ignored cops. They thought that they did not need them.

Dangerous areas knew that they needed cops,

Using my cellphone memory, I called an inside number for NYC Department of Transportation Potholes Crew, known as "the Hairy and Tarry Team."

After some Civil Service banter, a truck promised to come fill up this pothole before next week.

So I accomplished something.

Breathing out happier, I kept farming the concrete.

Eddie went past, hauling a six-pack of beer under a flabby arm.

"Officer, can I ask you a question?" a barfly-type woman asked, weaving a bit on cheap red sneakers with gray tape across one toe.

"Yes, my beatnik."

"Have you ever shot anyone?"

We cops got that question every so often. It seemed to dominate conversation.

"Have yourself a pleasant evening, young lady," I managed to say.

"Naw, you can tell me, I won't tell anyone else."

"Because of our deep personal relationship?"

She went a-sailing on her carefree way.

A blue-and-white eased up the block, saw me and kept going.

Either they thought that Manhattan North Patrol Borough had assigned extra cops like me here or that my CRIT tale about a sting here had already taken root. I hoped that it was the CRIT rumor moving fast.

CHAPTER 19.

The next day at eleven, I walked past the Dunkin' Donuts on First Avenue. Smells of coffee and hot bacon sandwiches tempted me.

The freckle-faced dog walker, the gitta-mort man who griped about potholes, was walking the same Jack Russell terrier.

"Hello again," I said.

He looked me over. Someday soon some fanatic collector was going to spot my shield as a fake but so far the surrounding uniform made it look real.

"Yar," he contributed.

"That pothole you showed me?" I said. "I phoned it in. DOT will fill it in this week."

"Yar. You called at night?"

His tone made me step back. He sounded like I was lying.

"Some cops have an inside line," I said. "Not for the public. And those guys ride all night."

"DOT?"

"Sure," I faked a laugh. Somehow, he had me backing up. "Remember those trucks tarring roads and jamming traffic on the FDR Drive at three in the morning? That's our tax dollars paying DOT."

He nodded, sniffed and walked his dog away.

My thigh muscles tensed, bulging out the blue uniform pants. The sawed-off bobbed a bit in the surgical wrap.

"He think that I'm jiving," I said aloud, to cool myself down. "He is acting like I never called DOT. Is that what ComPol does to people?"

He was still ankling down the avenue.

"I should walk up one side of his ass and down the other," I said. "Turkey letter-writing, typical civilian fool."

I shook my head to cool it down.

My sneakers rasped the sidewalk some more.

Night quieted the street.

I plodded along, fighting the melancholies.

"You are so stupid! You are screwing up my life!" some man shouted behind me.

His tone called the cop in me.

He sounded choking mad and out of control.

I turned to see a burly office-worker type with departing gray hair and a moustache slinging a young woman down a building's front stoop. She covered her face with her hands. Built as thickly as he was, she skipped backwards up the stoop, face crumpling, about to cry.

"Why did you tell them that?" he ranted. "That's my own personal business!"

"I didn't," she said.

"A-HEM!" I said as loudly as I could.

The man looked me over.

"You want something?" he asked.

"A moment of your time, good sir," I said.

"You're a wise guy?"

"Card-carrying."

He stepped closer to me. My feet skittered backwards a foot.

"Pardon the cliché," I said.

"She's my daughter," he said. "And she's lying on me to some creeps out to screw me."

"How misguided they must be," I said. "How old is she?"

"That's your business?"

"Government says that it is," I said. "You can discipline your own child, within reason, if she's a minor. Unless she's an emancipated minor."

The daughter shook her bright blonde head, pug-nosed and broad, at me.

"It's okay, cop," she said. "I'm nineteen."

"What year? Quick!"

"I'm nineteen."

"You look seventeen to me," I said. "That's a minor. You just failed my standard test. Why don't you show me some ID?"

"I'm disciplining my daughter and you got no reason to interfere without a warrant," the man said. "How about I report you for harassing me? I can call your Internal Affairs."

"That's like whistling," I said. "Anyone can whistle."

"I got no ID," she said.

"Yup," I said, watching the man's fat hands squeezing into fists. "My name's Max," I said to the girl. "What's yours?'

"Don't tell him!" the man said.

"That's all I need, sir, to arrest you for OGA," I said, breathing out and trying to nerve up for some scuffling. "Obstruction of Governmental Administration.'

He charged.

My fear forced me backwards. He followed me. He went off-balance. I grabbed his shoulders and drew back. He went into the garbage cans, flopped and dropped down. The garbage cans WHANGED!

"Stay low!" I said.

He got hands on the concrete, pushing himself up. I stepped on the hand.

"Awww!"

I kept my foot on it.

"You want to fight me?" I asked. "Maybe with a broken hand? Lie down and stay there."

"I'll report you!"

"From inside jail? Hop to it. Who tried bum-rushing me? Look around you."

A few beatniks stopped, watching us play.

"You, young lady," I said. "What's your name?"

"Thalia."

"Thalia, you're not in any trouble from me. But to help you, I need your name."

"It's Maynard. But my dad is Mitchell Kimbry."

Kimbry tried getting up again.

I just put more weight on his hand.

"You can't stop me from disciplining my own daughter!"

"I got you pinned, pal, and that's a gray legal area. Want to debate it in the pen at Central Booking? Thalia, my dear, do you have any bruises from him?"

She did not react.

"Thalia?"

She nodded.

Kimbry writhed. I leaned more. He yelped.

"But you can't see the bruises anymore," she said. "They all faded."

"It's nice to see real white trash still existing in the Play-pen," I said. "We cops tend to focus on other groups. But you're still here on rent-control, aren't you, Mitchell Kimbry?"

"I'll get you fired!"

"That's tougher than you could imagine. But, okay. I'm on rent-control, too."

They looked at me as if I had snapped my cap.

"Thalia, my dear, what's your address?"

She paled.

"422 East 83rd," she said. "Right here, apt 2C."

"Thank you. Does he use you for sex?"

Kimbry kicked out. But I was waiting and dodged it. Then I dropped my weight onto his back and kept him pinned. I twist-locked his right wrist back and frisked him with my free hand.

"No," she said. "I won't let him do that. And he's too scared to try. He's a fraidy-cat."

"Okay," I said. "Mr. Kimbry, you just swung on a cop. Would you like to sleep in the joint?"

"I don't care!"

"I let you up, we chalk this to experience. You get a beer and a bath for your hand and go flop in your own bed. Or we go all legal-like. I say that you fell and I helped you up. What do you want?"

He heaved. His belly flopped. I was glad to see that his belly was bigger and softer than mine. Maybe next year, I would look like him.

"I'll make a complaint," he said.

But he was losing steam. We both knew it.

Street people lived and died for the moment.

His had passed.

"Kimbry, why don't we both keep lawyers out of our lives?"

His face twisted and slacked.

"No arrest, man. Let me up," he said. "It's not worth it."

"How true that is."

I stepped back, watching his hands. Stress sponged sweat through my uniform. I wanted this over before I fell apart.

Thalia was already walking away. She did not look back.

No law let me hold her.

"Kimbry, I don't care if she's your daughter. No more hitting her. If she has bruises, she can get you locked up. So don't do it. You're too smart for that. Right?"

"Yeah."

"I'll stop by apt 2-C whenever I want. And you'll let me in."

"You shit, man. Why I let you in?"

"Because if you don't, I'll feed you to the state hotline for possible minor abuse. They have more clout than us cops, can enter without a warrant, seize your child, interview your neighbors and co-workers and do all kinds of dancing on your head."

"But I don't abuse her!"

"I'm not sure. But this is how I check. We got a deal?"

He nodded.

He looked older and fatter now, aging rapidly.

"Cop can't interfere," a woman said across the street.
"Yes, he can," another one said. "And he's supposed to."
My beatniks were talking it up about me.
That was what I wanted.

CHAPTER 20.

By the next morning, I had just three days before CRIT started hunting me.

Leo gurgled over his morning coffee as I suited up again in the locker room.

When I reached 83rd Street, something felt different.

The beatniks looked at me a bit longer than they had yesterday.

They paused sweeping their stoops, walking their dogs or slowing their jogs into the cool-down period.

"Officer, what happened yesterday?" the Cheshire Cat woman with the missing front tooth asked me. "I saw you dealing with something."

Naturally, she would be the first one to ask me.

It was time for me to try distracting her.

"Naturally, I don't want this to damage our deep personal relationship," I began.

She gap-tooth smiled without thinking.

That was how she handled all questions.

"But I saw one person hit another and stepped in to find out why," I said.

"Can you do that?"

"Why do you ask?"

"Because most of the cops I see here just avoid working," she said. "We don't have much crime. So they get kind of lazy, I guess."

"This is the one of the safest precincts in the city," I said. "But you still find burglars and muggers working to take what you got."

She focused on the metal name-tag stamped "Royster" on my left chest over the fake shield.

"So, why did you step in?" she asked.

"Because I needed to find out what was happening."

"It was a father disciplining his child."

"It could have been anything. A mugging or a date-rape gone wrong. Or she might have been a sex worker trying to break free. Thousands of them exist here, even in this modern city with all attendant wonders."

"When you found it was family, you should have stopped."

"I'm enjoying our talk. What's your name, please?"

"Samantha. But all my close friends call me 'Sam,' and my closest, tightest, most intimate friends call me 'Sammie'."

"Nice to know," I said.

We appraised each other.

"Samantha, families sometimes break the law and abuse each other. Think back on your own family."

"I'd rather not."

"You see? Yesterday, I had to find out. What if I ignored them, kept walking to the doughnut shop, and he threw her out a third-story window? What would you think of us cops? Shouldn't I have done something to learn what was what?"

She smiled, making sure that we could talk again.

"And what did you find out?" she asked.

"Samantha, I want everyone on the block to come to me if they have a problem," I said.

She cocked her head and smiled.

Oh, no. Community policing, I thought.

"And when that happens, I will speak with you in private about the problem," I went on. "Nobody else will know unless you let me tell them."

"Like a shrink."

"One that you pay for with your taxes," I said. "If you let me, I'll refer your trouble to the right agency. Or step in myself."

"I read about something like that in *The Post*. It's a new kind of policing work, I bet."

"You'd bet wrong. It's not new. Some call it Community Policing. But Community Policing is just a fraud designed to waste time and accomplish nothing. What you and I are agreeing to do is just old-fashioned commonsense policing. Like a cheer. 'Beatniks for Max!'"

"I guess," she said. "Okay. See you later."

When I finished with Samantha-the-Badge-Bunny, it was after 9:00 a.m. I turned down the fake radio calls on my cellphone, called Child Protective Services, and reported yesterday's family scene.

Reporting Daddy Kimbry held risks for me. But I was still a cop under oath to refer family problems to CPS.

Without giving my name, I made sure that the caseworker on the desk got all the details and would send an investigator on a home visit.

If I identified myself, they might check. My whole hustle would crumble.

If the daddy accused me of breaking our deal and making the call, I could say that some neighbor must have phoned.

Others broached the same subject throughout the day. I repeated the same line that I gave Samantha.

"You know, we need that kind of attention here," one dog-walking career-type woman said, letting her poodle befoul a tree-box. "Everyone thinks that nothing happens here. But a laid-off worker, a woman about 23, could not make her rent here. So she started breaking into apartments last year."

"Nobody wants to be evicted," I said.

"This was her way out of it. She did this for months. She even violated the apartments in her building. We asked for more protection. But they sent a lazy opinionated boor of a sergeant to explain why they could not do it."

"What happened?"

"We started watching ourselves. Someone noticed that she always went out empty-handed and came back with full pillowcases about an hour later."

"Clumsy. She should have carried an empty duffle bag. But burglars who do not plan ahead use their victims' pillowcases."

"We kept watching her. She went into another building and came out on the fire escape. We called 911. She tried telling you cops that she lived there. But we wised you up. You found a regular marketplace in her apartment. TVs, DVDs. Jewelry. Laptops."

"That kind of communicating helps everyone," I said.

"You think so?" she sniffed. 'It feels like we did all the work that you cops should do. Without pay."

☙

The clouds smeared oily gray above all of us. A wind riffled past the tiny shops below the sidewalk level.

Beatniks grouped in pairs watched me and talked.

A tall shape came up the block from First Avenue. He was a rangy youngster about 30, in a T-shirt and jeans.

He looked like my own sketch of the Horn Bug.

My head snapped down.

Moving too fast, my fingers tore a piece off the sketch Xerox.

Now the sketch looked different from the man in front of me.

But that night in the brownstone came back to me. Something about this man on the sidewalk recalled that lithe burglar running from the brownstone.

He might be my Horn Bug.

Tailing someone by yourself was tough. Try doing it in uniform, without anyone noticing.

Remembering the rules from the Hardy Boys Detective Handbook, I let him drift in front of me and then angled myself to his right rear. Most people checked for a tail over their left shoulder.

Beatniks held down their posts along 83rd Street, gabbing with each other. Hopefully, none would notice me tailing him.

This man's blondish hair was cut short, almost in a crew cut. He looked like he was in athletic shape, about six feet three and about 170 pounds. He wore an expensive red T-shirt and tailored Levi blue jeans. His large hands held no rings, wristwatches or bracelets. Jewelry was often as good as photos for identification, because men usually wore it in the same way for years.

He looked like someone who hit the gym regularly. I reminded myself to start hanging out near Crunch, Boom Fitness and the other gyms in the area.

My breath came out in spurts.

The sawed-off strapped to my thigh grew heavier.

He turned onto Second Avenue, went into a stationery and party store and came out with *The New York Times*. If he was the Horn Bug, he was an intellectual one.

Second Avenue sounded like a traffic madhouse. He winced and walked to East 82nd Street and turned left.

I stayed about sixty feet behind him, trying to look aimless.

He walked to First Avenue and turned left, looking around him on the sidewalks. That made me stay away.

He paced to East 83rd Street and the block that he had left.

Maybe he had spotted me. Or maybe he was just stretching his legs. Playpenners sometimes circled their own blocks and decided to change their clothes because of the weather.

If I got closer and made a sure ID, I would not try calling 911. Explaining myself would take forever. And Captain Day would reward any cop who tossed me into Bellevue ahead of schedule. They would be telling stories about Royster and his toy shield wherever cops beered up together.

If he was the Horn Bug, I would follow him into a doorway, lift the shotgun from my leg brace and order him to freeze. He could be carrying the same murder knife.

If he moved with the knife or went for a gun, I would blow his legs into pudding with the shotgun. Smart cops have learned not to try wrestling with a knife man. The odds were that a knife would cut an artery before any bullet stopped him.

"If he has a knife and menaces you with it, bury him," our academy trainers had said.

He turned back onto East 83rd.

I counted to five with a shaking voice. Then I fast-walked up to the corner.

He was not there.

Nothing but dog-walkers getting off the sidewalk before the rain hit.

My possible Horn Bug had gone into any of a dozen stores or buildings.

The super with the Slavic accent was standing out front, sucking smoke from a broken cheroot in his mouth. Gambling everything, I would have to trust him. But if he knew the Horn Bug, he might warn him that I was watching him. The Horn Bug would leave New York forever.

I would rot in Bellevue.

"Excuse me, sir," I said. "That man in the red T-shirt, just came around the corner? You saw him?"

"Sure. I watch everyone. Like I tell you," he said.

"Which place did he go into? Store or building?"

The super shrugged.

I stepped back and shook my head. My hat felt loose.

"Let's get this straight," I said. "Which one did he go into?"

"I'm not – I don't remember."

"I think that you do," I said, without thinking.

"I just kind of see him, you know? But I don't want involve, this business –"

"What 'business?'" I said. "He just dropped his wallet on the avenue. I need to return it to him,"

"Show me wallet, first."

"What?"

"Where he drop wallet?"

I stepped closer to him, in boxer stance.

"I'm telling you what happened!" I tried saying it quietly. "Let's not play mind games here. Where did he go?"

He decided. His eyes shuttered.

"I don't know," he said. "Somewhere. He went somewhere."

"ComPol fails again," I said. "Thanks for nothing."

I kept watching the line of buildings and shops that he could have entered. With his speed and pace, there were seven shops and three apartment buildings as possibles.

Time dragged past.

Feeling naked, I trudged past the doorway and stores where the Funny Bunny could have gone.

None of the stores showed his frame.

There was one toy store that I could not check. The sign outside read "Youth At Play." The front door was locked.

It looked dank and depressing. The store was another Playpen survivor, living on rent control. Like I was.

Any child browsing for toys here might suffer nightmares.

But I would have to check it out when it opened.

A few citizens went by, looked me over and probably thought about yesterday with Daddy Kimbry.

The clouds opened.

Rain lanced down.

Stepping into a deep doorway across the street, I kept watching.

Windows closed down along the block. Beatniks caught in the rain shielded their hair-dos with folded newspapers and plastic shopping bags held in their hands.

The rain turned wild.

I remembered the murder scene.

The wind ruffled garbage piled outside the stoops.

Shoppers left the shops.

Then the store-keepers locked up for the night and headed for the subway station at 86th Street. They hunched under umbrellas as they walked.

By my watch, three hours went by.

It was after nine.

The Horn Bug might be visiting a fair virgin to prepare her for life's great stage. He might not leave the apartment for the next few days.

The August rainstorm kept pelting down.

After more than five hours, I slumped back to Leo's garage and my nap on the couch there.

CHAPTER 21.

The next morning, I got the worrying willies enough to roll out off the floor early, into uniform and onto 83rd Street.

Time was running from me.

Foot-patrolling near Lexington Avenue and 83rd Street, I kept pushing one foot in front of the other.

At Second Avenue, the sedate brownstones ended. The tenements began.

Supers hosed down the sidewalks in front of gnarly door fronts.

You could smell wet concrete mixed with the tuna-and-onion smell of garbage ripening in the heat.

Today would be a sweaty dog day on East 83rd Street.

It would be a good idea for me to savor the air and sky. Soon I might be locked down behind chicken wire in a cell.

Miracle of miracles, the same beatnik who had refused to point out the suspect's store yesterday, stood on First Avenue. He chattered on his cellphone about Sissie messing up last night's drinking at the Tin Lizzie.

Forming a presence to intimidate him, I stood by until he finished.

He looked me over, standing there in uniform. He wanted to keep me waiting. It made him feel big.

His talk dragged on.

It took him forever to finish.

"How are you today?" I asked when he was folding up the phone.

"Yeah."

"You know that I'm trying to make this street safer," I said. "Truth and justice, you know?"

"Man, that's why you push us. You cops. Talk truth and justice shit. You just don't goddamn care."

He lost me with that kind of talk.

"No time for philosophy today," I said. "Memory any better?"

"Leave me alone, huh? All your bullshit."

"Be delighted to. Just one thing. Where did that joker go yesterday? That's all I need to know."

"You will beat me? You beat Kimbry."

I blew out a breath.

ComPol lay a-bleeding.

"Nobody beat anybody," I said. "He can't brutalize his own child. That leads to the kid beating him up in later life. Would you want your kid to do that?"

"My kids do that to me, I just shoot them."

"Ah, a family man."

"Huh?"

"Maybe you're too dumb to talk to," I said. "So we'll play it another way. Where did he go yesterday?"

"Man, why do you care so much? What's it to you?"

"Maybe he owes me money."

"And maybe I don't get involved. You don't understand people. That's why nobody trusts cops."

My leg muscles tensed. The sawed-off shotgun bobbed under the baggy pants.

I measured him like a butcher choosing where to cut a white-faced Hereford. A left jab would back him up for a right cross and then some left hooks to the gut would drop him onto his own sidewalk.

He read my face.

He walked away and into a newspaper store on First Avenue.

Maybe he wanted witnesses to whatever I was planning to do with him.

"There goes another happy ComPol customer," I said.

I tried to talk away my mad. Visions of green pastures, pretty butterflies and Jody's face flew me before me.

It was the right time to call Jody.

ꕤ

"You sound draggy," Jody said when I called her. "Are you starting to realize that this is a James Bond fantasy that you can catch him this way?"

"Thanks for the encouragement. Today, I'm going to find out where my possible Horn Bug went yesterday."

"You're not even sure that he is the Horn Bug. Why are you gambling on this one idea?"

"What else should I gamble on?"

ꕤ

One of the buildings had foreign letters cut into the stone. It took me a minute to recognize the letters as coming from the Czech alphabet. The polyglot mass of Hungarians, Germans, Irish and Czech had left their mark on the Playpen streets.

Tiny stores still hung on, ignoring the huge rents paid by newcomers.

One sold fresh-baked bread, another mailboxes and trinkets from India. I entered both, introduced myself as Max the local beat cop and watched the workers wait for me to leave. They had never heard of ComPol.

All the apartments had locked vestibules. I checked each for anything that might lead me to the Horn Bug but there was nothing. Yesterday's lead was dying fast.

Feeling small and lonely, I called Lipkin, my big brother figure.

"Have you wised up yet?" he asked. "Tell me where you are. I can pick you up in an hour, bring you into CRIT and protect you that way. Otherwise, come Labor Day, you're a fugitive."

"Does surrendering help me?"

"Sure it does. They might release you on your own recognizance."

"That's for perps, Al. They can't do that for a mental patient involuntary lockdown."

"They can do what they want," Lipkin said. "Just like an adult Max."

"That's what my PBA lawyer said. Later, maybe."

"'Later, maybe' is going to be too late."

ɞ

The toy store was set below the sidewalk level. The words "Youth At Play" were painted on a sign above a darkened window. You could not see much from the sidewalk.

Stepping down the six steps, I paused at the store window to let whoever was inside see my summer uniform. Then I pushed the door open.

Stacks of toys in lay on display. The store was small, about twenty-five feet long by fifteen feet wide. Toy stores were not my territory for the past four decades. But I would never squire my kids to shop in this dump. It looked like a front, a place to score anything illegal. Gambling action, illegal massages with a happy ending or a place where I could buy another piece under the table.

"Good morning," I said as cheerfully as possible. "My name's Max, and I'm new on the beat. How are you today?"

More ComPol nonsense, I thought.

The woman behind the counter nodded and coughed a smoker's cough. You could smell the stale cigarettes. She probably was too lazy to go upstairs and out to smoke. I could not see healthy Playpen mamas who jogged and played tennis bringing their kiddies here to enjoy secondhand smoke.

She nodded a head covered by an orange kerchief, looking like a crow. She mumbled something that I could not catch.

"Since I'm new here,' I prattled on, "I was wondering if there was anything that I could help you with. Maybe something that the other cops forgot to do?"

Always let the taxpayer gripe, that was my ComPol motto.

"Is okay," she said, like someone not wanting to talk.

But I was the vacuum cleaner for ComPol so I fixed a jolly smile on my mug.

"The sale begins when the customer says 'no,'" I muttered.

"What?"

"Nothing."

"The noise, you know," she said. "The kids."

"Sure."

I sounded like a game-show host.

"But you can't do nothing about that, huh?" she asked.

"Send them all to summer camp."

"Well, summer's almost over."

"Don't remind me," I said. "How long have you had this store?"

She bobbed her head and did not answer.

Too long, I thought to myself.

This was going nowhere fast.

"Thank you for your time," I said. "Like I said, my name's Max."

Turning to leave, in my creaky uniform, I stepped back to the door and sunlight.

She got up from her stool. The light hit her.

Her body stretched. She stood tall and thin, about four inches under my six feet.

I grunted in surprise.

"Yeah?" she asked.

My Horn Bug was also tall and slim, almost spidery, without any fat on him.

"Summer cold, that's all," I said. "Pollen, maybe. Good-bye, ma'am. What's your name, by the way?"

She did not answer me.

I kept going up the stairs and into the street.

Her size and shape reminded me of the Horn Bug. She could be his family. She could be his mother.

CHAPTER 22.

After I switched out of uniform, I went to an Information Services, Inc., a company that promised to dig up everything possible on the Youth At Play store and the characters working there. For a fee, they promised to make happy with all their data. Passing over my Visa card for payment, I wondered if I was losing my own mind.

Logically following that thought, I plodded to a building that looked like a medieval castle on West 79th Street and Broadway and buzzed Dr. Clarkwall.

"Well, well," he said at his door. "The guardian."

"Twenty minutes of your time, Doctor. And not to discuss my own case history, but somebody else."

"My time goes high, Max. Why should I give it away?"

"Because I took the rap for you back at Saint Blaise's School For Young Men on stealing the chapel tapestry, got suspended and went through a nice bit of hell in those days."

Dr. Clarkwall looked better tended that I did, with a relaxed and cheerful look to him. A light gray summer suit went with his light blue shirt and quiet tie. His brown leather shoes and belt matched. His hair flowed in a discreet razor cut.

My schoolboy memory did not seem to rattle him.

I lay on the venerable couch that his psychiatry patients used and described everything that I knew about the Horn Bug.

Rising, I got the walking handshake that ended at the door.

"I heard about this killing on TV, of course," he said. "Will they make you a detective if you solve it? I'll do a spot of research and call you soon."

"Sooner rather later, Doctor. Please. Tempus is a-fidgeting."

☙

"Coffee, if you please," I asked Lila.

She looked over the other customers at me in the uniform and did not seem to focus.

"Max, remember?" I prompted. "Local servant of truth and justice?"

She bobbed her head.

"Coming right up," she said.

"No hurry, beatnik," I said. This was no time to rush anybody.

The inside of the Java Janey's was packed with Playpenners seeking a bargain breakfast in the land of trendy boutique appetizers. They scanned their folded *Times* while slurping their morning liquids and comfort victuals.

"This is an interesting street," I said. "On the surface, ritzy and comfortable. But there are still lots of folks just hanging on."

"Like me," Lila said.

"Go into some of the stores and you're back in 1899," I said. "With brick dust everywhere and no indoor toilets."

"If you got a vivid imagination."

"Then I must have. That's what turned me into a cop. I kept imagining that what I do would make a difference."

"Keep imagining that," Lila said. "I used to work with Special Ed kids, trying to keep them happy and functioning."

Customers pled for attention to their home fries.

"That's a heartbreaker," I said. "Did you ever bring them to that toy store down the block?"

"Which toy store?"

"'Youth At Play,'" I said. "A wild title, if ever I heard one."

"Is that still open? They open and close all the time."

"Well, maybe they keep getting arrested or something," I said, taking my coffee. "How many work there?"

"Some unhealthy family, I think. I can't keep track of them."

"Beats the hell out of me, too," I said. It was time to roll some dice here. "Doesn't her son and daughter help her out there?"

"I don't know."

I made a face and sucked down the coffee that tasted too bitter now.

All I had was someone who looked like the Horn Bug near that store. And the owner looked like him, slim and blonde and tall.

"D'you know their names in that store?" I asked.

Lila blew out a strand of hair out of her mouth.

"What happened when you hit that father down the block?" she asked.

That stopped me.

"I didn't hit anyone," I said. "Necessary force had to be used to stabilize the situation."

'You should hear how you talk."

"I need some support here," I said. "A cheer. Something like 'Beatniks, for Max!'"

She did not repeat my cheer.

She tossed her head and walked away.

☙

In my notebook, I scribbled down about a dozen different addresses in the precinct. Then I wrote in the address of the toy store as 378 East 83rd.

Lipkin answered his cellphone, subway noise in the background.

"Are you ready to start acting smart?" he asked. "Getting yourself out of the trouble that your wisecracking got you into?"

"Get me some who-what-where on these addresses and we'll dicker some more," I said.

"You're trying to con an old con man."

Trying to speak clearly over street noise, I fed him the addresses.

"One of these is the real deal," he said. 'The others are just to throw me and the other adults off while you play Peter Pan and refuse to grow up."

"This protects you, Al. Nobody can stake out a dozen locations at the same time."

"I'm still a Civil Servant, Max. Under the regs, if a boss asks me to re-count this conversation today, I have to obey and give him everything. Think about that."

I ended the call and folded up the phone.

The heat was crawling inside my uniform. The sawed-off shotgun started itching against my calf. Someday it might loosen and fall off with a clatter on the sidewalk.

ଓ

On Second Avenue, a reedy black man was bouncing on one foot to the other, with a broad palm outstretched.

"Spare any change, spare any change?" he kept chanting to the Playpenners hustling past, speaking into their phones.

He did not see me.

Reaching into my pocket, I turned down my cellphone broadcasting the radio runs.

The Playpenners saw me approaching him and took time to watch our little drama unfold. ComPol was about to try again. He looked like about five years older than my forty-six, taller and in better shape, like everyone else in the Playpen.

A dusty denim jacket with bulging side pockets hung over torn tan khakis and sneakers. Those pockets worried me.

"Spare any change?" he asked.

"Afternoon, sir," I said, approaching from his rear left, the safest angle. "You see any suspicious characters around here?"

He bobbed his skeletal head.

"Yessir," he said. "Sir, I just lost my bus ticket from Ludowici, Georgia, late last night and don't have any –"

"Save it for the rookies. Do I look young enough to fall for that one?"

"I got the receipt."

His hands went into his pockets. I half-turned, hands already in position.

"Stop! Don't take those hands out," I said, trying to put steel in my tone. "Keep them where they are. Or else, you're going down."

He gaped at me.

Traffic sluiced by on Second Avenue.

A blue-and-white NYPD car was going downtown. The driver saw me and the panhandler and slowed, drifting near. His emergency lights flicked on.

That was what I did not want.

The driver was a Latino sergeant. I'd never seen him before.

The car words read "32 Precinct." He was out of his turf. He did not know my face. Unless Lieutenant Lenny of CRIT had put a wanted flyer out for me already.

The good sarge was probably just heading downtown, to kill some time at court, in the highest tradition.

"Okay, sir," I said, chopping my words short from jitters. "Start stepping."

With street smarts, he sensed something wrong.

"Look, officer –"

"Move it!" I said. "Or else we start checking for warrants. Today's your lucky day."

The sarge was getting closer.

"I'm just trying to explain," my new pal said.

He knew that I was trying to dump him away.

His team always wanted to mess up my team. Right now was no different. He stood his ground.

"What have you got?" the sarge asked.

His car stood ten feet from me. If he was sharp and got a good look at my toy shield, the comedy would crumble.

"Just a skell," I said, relying on cop shorthand for "a skeleton, someone better off dead."

My panhandler decided to take exception to my tone.

"Now, wait a minute, officer," he said. "I offered to show you my bus ticket receipt from Ludowici, Georgia, for $119.46 but you just go all hard-head with me and I'm a Vietnam veteran –"

"Cue the organ. Take off."

He still hesitated.

Behind me, the car door opened and shut. The sarge was taking positive police action.

I wheeled around and jay-walked across Second Avenue traffic. The sarge could inherit my little street scene here. Maybe he and the panhandler could bond over something.

Cars screamed at me and slammed to a stop.

"Hold on, officer!" the sarge shouted.

I had to turn my head and look back.

A taxi almost hit my gunbelt but skewed sideways.

The sarge wore a pointed little moustache, slim runner's build and a pained look on his face.

He did not know what to do.

That was what I wanted.

As a boss, he did not want to know some things. If I was goofing off with my sergeant's permission, this sarge from the Three-Two might get punished for upsetting our deal.

Maybe he thought that I was some stray cop, shaking people down. My panhandler would surely part with twenty or fifty bucks to avoid a collar.

"I'm talking to you!" he shouted.

"Come on, sarge," I said to myself. "Of all the times to get conscientious."

When I reached the curb, I turned right and started walking uptown. The traffic should block the sarge from following me.

Across the avenue, I saw him lift the portable radio and then belt it again. My panhandler was distracting him, waving his arms.

The sarge ignored him and moved back into his car. The emergency lights came back on.

His car lurched away from the curb.

By now, I was a block away.

But he could box me in.

At 84th Street, I turned left.

He backed his car up towards me.

This was getting worse.

A double-parked truck blocked him.

"Hurray for the Playpen," I grunted.

A garage door yawned to my right.

I stepped into it.

A blubbery Latino joker with a handlebar moustache folded his *El Ocero* newspaper and eased up from his chair.

"Yessir, Officer?"

"See any kids run past here?" I asked. "Carrying a cell-phone, maybe?"

He pretended to think it over.

My shoes tapped the concrete.

"Sometime today, huh?" I said.

"What you say?"

"Let me take a look. You got a door to the service area in back of here?"

He thought that one, too.

The sarge was getting closer.

"Never mind," I said, moving past. "Where's your back door?"

He pointed with a bristly chin covered with fever sores.

I strode back from the street, found the door and yanked it open.

A narrow walkway of concrete ran around the building. A scrappy tree survived against the back of an apartment building.

I slipped off my hat to make it harder for anyone to see me.

Another wire fence blocked me in.

I got behind the tree to hide.

Someone had thrown up nearby.

You could smell it.

I waited and waited for the sarge to come through that door after me.

My ribs kept heaving under the blue tunic.

CHAPTER 23.

When I finished my day of hardball street policing, I limped back to Leo's garage and stripped off the uniform.

Leo brought me my civilian clothes, across the street and barked Spanish at another super. The super led us to an apartment being renovated. I used my shower-and-shave pocket kit in the new bathroom.

The supers and street people dealt out favors in their own world, ignoring the rich tenants.

"This renovate cost about a cool mil," Leo said. "Is not necessary. They say they just like new things."

"That's Playpen nervousness," I said. "And this tenant has the cash to indulge it."

Hot water blasted me.

Leo handed me one of the tenant's monogrammed towels. I stepped naked and wet from the shower.

"You don't look too good," Leo said.

"You're being kind. I look terrible. Your floor is no four-poster bed."

Leo looked hurt.

"I sleep all the time, the floor," he said.

"Yeah, but you're usually too drunk to hit the ground with your hat."

"Sometimes," he said, grinning. "But these times, I don't remember."

I dried my body, shaved and dressed in street clothes. They felt light and easy.

On the way out, I threw the super some dinner cash.

☙

I followed Leo back into his garage.

"Leo, I'm all wired up."

"Hard day, the office?"

"Time for some civilization and its softening effects. Keep your eye on my locker, Leo. My whole life is in there.'

"My whole life inside this smelly garage."

Balling up my uniform, I brought it to another dry-cleaner off Third Avenue. To avoid Lieutenant Lenny of CRIT doing a manhunt, I would have to keep switching dry-cleaners.

I had to avoid the ones used by the One-Nine cops. That meant using the more expensive ones, west of Second Avenue. NYPD cops shunned extra expenses. That is why a lot of us looked like circus clowns playing cops.

☙

Something soft inside me pointed me towards Hunter College and Professor Jody.

For some reason, her schedule had stayed inside my brain-box. Today, she had another class ending at ten.

All day long, I had been moving and staking the block out. It was time to start staking out Jody.

Waiting near the Hunter College plaza on Lexington Avenue, I sank onto a molded concrete bench and tried to re-knit myself.

College kids broke free from the building and snapped out cigarettes and foreign talk. They fortified themselves for a sub-way trek home. With Playpen rents, nobody taking Hunter classes could afford to live within five subway stops of the school.

Part of me yearned to flop back to sleep at Leo's garage again. The other part yearned to see Jody's face and eyes.

She came outside with that off-gait step that I recognized by now. Her pale lipstick mouth opened a bit seeing me.

"What's the deal here?" she asked in her breathless way. "Am I going to have to scan the street, watching out for you every night?"

"Probably not next week."

"What if I get some normal man to take me out to dinner and quiet talk? Like regular people do, Max."

I smiled.

"I do believe that you are remonstrating me, Professor. While utilizing my Christian name. How sweet."

She wore a purple blouse that somehow meshed with her lipstick color. Her tanned skin hinted that she had been beaching recently. Her jeans were dark blue and tailored. Painted pink toes peeked from antique leather sandals.

"May we tango tonight, Professor?"

"Please tell me why."

"Because this might be our last tango in the Playpen."

"Why?"

"You may have forgotten, but I cannot. I am due to start serving a sentence to prove my mental health next week."

"Don't be a martyr, Max. I already told you to leave New York."

"As I said, running will make it a criminal case. They'll slap a felony warrant on me, put it in their computers and stop my ATM and credit cards. It might take them a week to roll me up and into the crazy house."

଼

We sat at a table outside Sessions 73. She had slipped out of her sandals and curled her feet underneath her. That intrigued me.

She ordered a gin Martini, looking wicked as she did it.

A braised swordfish with black olive rice followed. She downed a second Martini with her dinner. That made me grin over my Maker's Mark Bourbon and Salade Niçoise.

She was planning to enjoy her liquor tonight. That would help my hustle.

"Why do we suffer this thick wall of miscommunication between cop and citizen?" I asked.

"You already asked me that. Repeating yourself gets dull."

"Jody, nobody whom I know has your wit. And that's what I need tonight."

Liquor better help me with this, I thought to myself. Because it is a thin hustle that I am trying to run.

"Silly. Everyone wants cops to prevent crime, keep their block safe and not violate anyone's rights while they're doing that," Jody said. "They want to breathe free without having to fear either crook or cop."

"But like all workers," I said, "cops withdraw into their cocoon of dodging arguments, work or unreasonable bosses. The service suffers. Then we add in the element of risk and the capability of using force to protect themselves. Season that with snap-second decisions about race, class and power-mad supervisors holding your family hostage because of the pension and you have a very complex set of difficulties. It's no wonder that dysfunction occurs."

"It's occurring, all right," she said, ending that bit of conversation. "Shall we dance?"

On the dance floor, she fitted well against my left palm and the fingers of my right hand. A scent of patchouli wafted off her.

"This is part of the copera?" she murmured.

I let the silence build for a bit.

"They're about to push me out of where I'm flopping," I lied. "And our hero in this copera needs a place to rest his weary head."

"Didn't I tell you that I need to get to Italy on this sabbatical? Or else maybe lose my home?"

I spun her into a tango step called a gancho, where her leg hooked mine and did not answer. I fumbled the move.

"You'll never learn this dance," she said. "Don't you care about my house and my daughter? Or do you want to keep playing policeman?"

"'Playing policeman' is right," I said. "All right. Let's drop it. This Hardy Boy will get through somehow."

We danced some more.

"Why do new officers get paid only $25,000?" she asked. "That's poverty."

"Because the old-timers and the union sold the rookies out on the contract," I said. "The veterans enriched themselves. Like Congress does."

Jody was right.

The Argentine Tango kept eluding me. But the music and movement eased the lines on the face and creases in my mind.

"Maybe you're right about everything," I murmured into her neck.

"This is a school night," she said. "And it's too late for the subway. Do you have enough money for a cab? If not, I do. Somewhere in my purse."

"This Civil Servant can still afford a cab," I said. "So far."

Back outside on First Avenue, we tried panning the traffic stream for a Yellow Cab with the Free sign lit up on top.

Nothing appeared.

We ankled a block uptown.

A black man, wearing a T-shirt reading "Eat Ice Cream" and crusted blue jeans, held his hand out on the corner. Grayish whiskers clouded the scars on his face.

"Spare some change?" he crooned. "Come on."

He was ignored.

"I'm a soft-spoken man," he sang.

More Playpenners went past.

"Spare some change?" his voice rose.

"Here's part of your public," Jody said. "Are you two pals?"

"Not yet," I said.

Two well-suited professionals jostled past Mr. Ice Cream, the Soft-Spoken Man.

"Spare some change?"

"Aw, bite me," the larger one said, listing to his left.

"Just need a little bit of change."

"Fuck you. Get a job."

"Leave him alone, Wade," the other one said. "Why bother with him?"

"You got everything," Mr. Ice Cream said. "Can't you spare me a taste?"

"Drop dead," Wade, the larger one said.

Wade shoved him. Mr. Ice Cream went backwards against a parked car. It hurt my own lumbar discs to see it. He flopped to the ground. Wade stepped in and kicked a polished moccasin against his T-shirt.

"Oh, dear," I said. "Dear, dear me."

"You're ruining this city!" Wade shouted. "Everywhere I go, there's some scum like you wanting a handout!"

Wade was working himself up.

He kicked him again. I stepped closer.

"Excuse me, sir," I said. "You made your point. You can leave now."

'Or what?" Wade said.

He jabbed me. It stung my jaw.

I stepped in, took his right punch on my shoulder and grabbed his belt. He was already off balance. I went with his body weight, swirled him around and into the car's window.

Glass exploded with a WHUMF!

He went halfway into the car. Mr. Ice Cream rolled away. Wade cursed and pushed himself out of the car window.

"Call 911!" Jody said. She blocked Wade, buying me time. He shoved her into a garbage can.

His pal grabbed me around the neck. He tried to choke me. Bystanders shouted. Heels grated on the sidewalk.

I butted my head backwards twice against the pal's face.

My elbow sliced back into his gut. He buckled. His weight went against me. I left-hooked his gut. He gagged and threw up, just missing Jody.

Wade came back, blood running like syrup over his haircut. I leaned away and stretched and kicked as high as I could, like in the movies. My foot caught his chin and he spun around and dropped back on the sidewalk.

Mr. Ice Cream moaned to himself as he fingered Wade's wallet out of Wade's pants and plucked out the credit cards.

"Stop that!" Jody said.

"Re-distributing the wealth," I panted.

"Blood all over your face and you're still wisecracking," she said.

Mr. Ice Cream rolled to his feet like a teenager and was moving down the street, leaving this Manhattan vignette far behind him.

"Come, my flower," I wheezed. "Let us away."

"Shouldn't we do something?"

"Believe me, I did enough," I said.

Wade and Pal were lolling over the concrete.

"Real cops will be here soon enough," I said. "My standing around would only inhibit them."

I took her hand and guided her onto East 74th Street in front of a squat stone church. Sirens blared.

"Jan Hus Church right here," I said. "Perfect place to avoid my former colleagues. Note the sunken steps leading down."

"How did you know this was here?"

"When we were 15, my friend Ace and I used to slug down Ripple here."

"You became a cop after you grew up in this neighborhood?"

"I'm not sure that I ever grew up."

"Maybe it's a good time to start."

"I just schooled here, on scholarship. But I never bought into the Playpen white-man's-burden philosophy."

My breath scraped against my throat. It was another reminder how much I was out of shape.

More sirens screamed. Car doors slammed. Radio voices buzzed.

"Why did you get involved with those kids?" she asked.

"I should let them stomp a loser asking for change?"

"But don't you stop panhandlers on your beat?"

"Not that way," I said.

"Well, I think that there was another way to handle that."

"You're welcome to try."

I tried focusing on other things, like how Jody's face looked smooth and calm in the streetlamp glow.

"Now you see why I need shelter," I said. "I'm a marked man wherever I go in this Playpen."

She settled down on the steps. She looked up at the square gray bricks forming the church.

"What's that writing on the wall?" she asked.

"Czech. The Playpen used to have loads of Czech, Hungarians, Germans and Poles living here. My father lumped them all together and called them 'Dutchmen.'"

"Your father sounds colorful."

"Look who he raised."

I leaned against her, inhaling her patchouli fragrance.

The adrenaline dump took hold. Energy was running out of me like sand from a sock.

She must have felt the same way.

We leaned against each other.

"Part of me was rooting for you back there," she mumbled. "I wanted you to win."

My eyes closed.

Then I was somewhere else, half-awake and half-asleep.

Drifting and drifting, I kept my eyes closed.

My cellphone went off. It played "The Stars And Stripes Forever" by Sousa.

"Are we marching?" Jody mumbled.

Groggy, I fitted the phone to my ear.

"There's a new kill," Lipkin's voice said. "I hope to hell that you got an alibi for this afternoon."

"Why are you shouting at me?"

"You got to cover yourself, that's all I'm saying. Come into the precinct. Talk to the squad."

"Who got killed?" I asked.

Jody gasped.

"Another blueblood socialite woman," Lipkin said. "The media is already howling. TV camera crews everywhere. The Police Commissioner must be ready to hide under his bed."

"I've got an alibi," I said. "But it won't help me much."

"Somebody saw you somewhere?"

"Everybody saw me everywhere."

"Whatever that means," Lipkin said. "They're keeping me out because I'm your protector."

"If only they knew."

"Settle down, Max. But I know some of the team inside the scene. They talked to me. The killer cut open a window, went inside that way and tied her up. He raped her all kinds of ways. It went on for hours."

I dropped my head.

"Think how she felt," I said.

"I do."

"I should have been able to stop him by now," I said. "This ComPol, this Community Policing, is all a patent medicine magic show that accomplishes nothing. Nobody is helping me where I'm working."

"ComPol works sometimes. Maybe you're doing it wrong."

"Save it for the Academy, Al."

"The M.O. fits for your Horn Bug. But Hundshamer from CRIT is rolling over this way. He'll like you for this kill. If I know anything, he'll try to get some tame Assistant DA to put a warrant on you."

"For murder?"

"Not yet. Any felony charge will jail you while Hundshamer builds a murder case around you. Criminal Negligence is a nice catch-all charge."

I shook and got up from the church stone steps.

"You're down to the wire, Max," Lipkin said. "It's over."

"Not yet. Where did this murder happen?"

"I'm not telling you. Don't come here. Meet me at Neil's Coffee Shop on Lex and 70th and we'll go into the precinct together."

"Surrender myself, huh? That's what my lawyer advises."

"You should listen to him. You always said that you would listen to our PBA lawyer. Why are you breaking your own rules now?"

"I wish I knew. I didn't kill her, Al. Thanks for calling me."

I folded the phone and stared at it.

Then I looked back at Jody and flipped the phone open again. I started dialing as I paced along the street.

"One-Nine Precinct, Police Officer Nalbantian," a voice said after a few rings. "How can I help you?"

"This is Captain Crispin, Duty Captain for tonight," I said. "We're a little slow on that phone, Nalbantian. Is your sergeant available?"

All cops stuck on the desk soon learned to cover for their sergeants.

"Never mind that," I said, without giving him time to think. "I'm supposed to meet some idiot sergeant at this murder in your command. Damn fool gave me the wrong address. Where is it, Nalbantian?"

"Cap, the detectives got all that."

"Nal-bant-ian," I said, stretching out the name. "Just get me that address ASAP. Am I clear?"

It worked.

"168 East 71st Street, Captain."

"Let's see if we can stay on the ball, Nalbantian."

I folded the phone.

"Let's walk up to Second Avenue," I said. "I'll put you in a cab and give you cash to get home."

"There's another dead woman? You're going there?"

"There is and I am."

"Why? What can you possibly accomplish that others cannot? Didn't you tell me that your friend Al is a genius at murder scenes?"

"They won't let him in."

"But they'll let you poke around? Don't be a child again, Max."

"There will be a crowd outside this Playpen brownstone," I said. "Sex killers often hang around to appreciate the mess they made. It warms their Mister Happy. I can take pictures of the crowd with my cellphone."

"So can the police photographers who are there."

"But I'll know if anyone in the crowd lives or hangs on East 83rd Street. After the time I've spent there, I know all the regular faces. Nobody else can do that."

"Why don't you tell Al to take pictures and show them to you later?"

"I can't put him at risk like that," I said. "They could charge him with Obstruction, fire him and take his pension if they found out."

"I'm not going to go there and take pictures for you. They would spot me and my nervous self in a New York minute. My new life in Italy will go up in smoke."

"Then cab it on home, please. I need to work."

"No. It's too risky," she said. "Get me home, and you can stay with me."

That stopped my pacing.

"Say that again," I said.

"You can sleep on my floor, Mister Charmer. Just on the floor. No romance, please."

"I need more than just tonight."

She nodded. Her body swayed.

"Why do I feel like I'm buying a used car?" she asked.

"Busted-down jalopy. I wished that I had never turned cop. Now I'm a fugitive, facing life in an asylum."

"That's self-pity, Max. What do you want to do right now?"

"I want to find the Horn Bug."

"You're fixated like a little boy on this. But tonight you won't find him in my apartment among the tropical plants and the Henri Rousseau paintings."

"Let's start looking now. Together."

ଓ

A dour taxi driver ferried us to Jody's apartment in a tin box smelling of spilled sodas.

Jody's brownstone whispered with mysterious night noises.

We tiptoed around the rooms, trying not to wake her daughter.

Jody gave me two blankets and a hard pillow to make up a bed on the floor of her living room.

Rain started coming down hard on her windows.

I nightmared that I was trying to survive inside Bellevue Hospital's ward. In the dream, someone kept coughing. The wet cough spray hit my ear. Daytime TV sounds erupted. My bed was too small.

CHAPTER 24.

I woke as if someone had left a dead rat in my mouth while they fixed locomotives between my ears.

Heat already warmed Jody's brownstone. Sunlight fell upon the venerable wood of the floors and furniture.

Fresh coffee and biscuit aromas wafted through the air.

The mirror showed a bruise on my face from last night's left jab. My face ached.

"Breakfast!" Jody's voice called from downstairs.

I clumped downstairs, finger-combing my hair.

"How did you sleep?" Jody asked as I entered the kitchen.

She looked younger without makeup.

Music on the counter played Faure's "Pavane."

"Chastely," I replied. "The Hardy Boys would approve."

"My daughter is already off to school. Just as well. I did not have the guts to try and explain why a man that I did not know was sleeping in our living room."

"But you do know me well."

"Do I?"

Home-made biscuits, bacon and poached eggs and coffee coaxed me back to feeling. This was much better than Leo's garage.

After last night's perfume, she smelled like warm bread.

I reached up from the chair and hugged her.

She stopped, then put her arms around me and hugged me back.

Then she broke the hug and looked at me.

"This doesn't mean anything," she said. "If you were a subway pillar or a bus-stop sign, I would have done that just the same way."

It seemed like a good time to shut up.

"Do you hear what I'm saying, Mister-About-to-Be-Locked-Down-for-Life?"

Her voice sounded shaky.

"I'm not getting involved with any more lost causes," she said. "Those days of idealism are dead. What do you think of that?"

"I think that you better practice your Italian."

ଓ

Trying to move to cover up the hurt, I took a shower, brushed my teeth and shaved with the stuff that Jody kept for guests who failed to ahead.

Then I jumped on my phone. The wonderful world-shaker Information Services Company had no news for me as yet. But the velvet voice of the firm's clerk assured me that they "were working towards a successful resolution very soon."

That resonated like money talking.

Lipkin sounded brusque on the phone, like when we first met when he was teaching courses at the Academy.

"What do you want now, Royster?"

"I just got through the newspapers on this murder," I said. "Mrs. Tracy Lowell, late of a brownstone on East 71st Street. *The Times* gives an article this size to a homicide?"

"Because it's a pricey location. You know that."

"And page two of *The Daily News*. *The Post* put it on the front. Leave it to *The Post*."

"The photos show her as a beauty who ran six times a week and attended every social function that you can't afford," Lipkin said. "Charity, too. She is the new martyr of Manhattan. The Mayor and the Commissioner are screaming for us to clear it yesterday and bring her back to life, running around the Central Park Reservoir like she did two days ago."

"That's pretty unrealistic."

"CRIT has taken over this homicide," he said. "That's rare, but it does happen. Nobody except CRIT can work it. That's because CRIT has convinced the brass that you did it."

"Where's their evidence?"

"When you flee and hide, they do not need much evidence. You're playing their game, Max. The bosses know that nothing ever leaks to the media from CRIT. If the word got out that an ex-cop was murdering socialites from his precinct, all of Manhattan would sit up in bed and scream."

"This is lynch mob thinking."

"So to guard against leaks, CRIT carries this case. Hundshamer runs that shop like it is his own personal U-boat. Nobody gets nothing. They all hate him."

"I'm glad that CRIT and I can agree on at least one thing."

"Captain Day of your One-Nine looks like he's about ready to Do-the-Honorable-Thing."

In cop-talk, 'Doing-the-Honorable-Thing' meant killing yourself.

"So you can't do anything?" I asked.

"I can do even less than that. The case has been CRIT-ted. Get clear of this and do some good for yourself."

ɞ

Manhattan professionals lived and died by their workbenches. So I walked by the Mercedes-Benz showcase sales near the Hudson River dressed in my Cancer Society Thrift-Shop best – a tan poplin jacket, blue chambray shirt, jeans and loafers and asked the receptionist for Mr. Boyd.

Randy Boyd came out of his office, toothy smile over his black face, moving as coltish as he had in City College on our boxing team.

"So cool to see you, Max. How was life as a Hong Kong chef?"

"Hard to describe in a word."

"The grapevine has you doing some pretty wild things. You boxed in Mexico?"

"Too stout for that, Randy. I managed young fighters in Guanajuanto. It was a better life."

"Here I am, still flogging German Mercedes hardware to the public."

"That's what I need your help on," I said. My silver toy shield flashed from the black leather case. For extra umph, I had jammed my old Parks & Recreation gym card with photo in the plastic sleeve next to the shield. "I'm a John Law now, Randy."

"You're a cop?"

"People always use that tone when I tell them that. It just kills my self-confidence."

"You're a cop? Civil Servant?"

"And dragging that piece of lumber behind me, on Life's great pathway."

"Aren't you way too old?"

"Once, at 22, I got wonderfully drunk."

"More than once, if I recall right," Randy said.

"But this time, I took a dare from a bully to take the test for the Job, as they call it. In capital letters. He said that he would score higher than I could. So I took it."

"Why didn't you join then?"

"The next day, I barely remembered taking the test. Didn't care, either. The city lost my papers. I did not care for the next 19 years. Then a cold winter froze my apartment. It struck me that I needed a Civil Service job with some healthy benefits."

All around us salesmen muttered into telephones.

"And I recalled that somewhere back in the past, I had taken a city test. Or maybe it was an LSD acid hallucination."

"Entirely possible," Randy said. "With you."

"So I sued the city for losing my test papers and rending my law enforcement career asunder. I acted as my own lawyer, hoping for a cash settlement. Instead, the judge ordered me onto the Job forthwith."

"And you've been making friends ever since."

"That's why I need a peek at your salesman's manual."

"Are you serious?"

"I tried being serious once. All I could get was construction work."

"Why my manual?"

"Because I must needs think creatively. We cops do not understand how to sell ourselves or our product."

"You mean Community Policing?"

"I spit in the milk of Community Policing. But you salesmen learn to sell things that customers do not really need. Or else you don't eat. I need to learn your tricks."

"Do you know what happens if we get caught letting the public read the big book?"

"Now, don't be a crepe-hanger, Randy. I just need some time alone with this Kama Sutra manual of Salesmanship. Chapters like 'How to Trim the Sucker without Him Hollering, 'Cop'."

"I wouldn't know how to work this, Max."

"Well, it's not espionage. Tell your boss that I want to buy a Mercedes. Right now. How much time will your boss give you alone with me?"

"Whatever it takes."

"Then close the door and break out that manual," I said, taking out my cellphone. "I'll photograph the pertinent pages with this, and no fool of a fathead boss will ever know."

"How did you know?"

"Know what?"

"That my boss is a fathead."

"He's a boss, isn't he? Let's get started on our espionage."

"And just why do you need to see this manual? What kind of case are you working on?"

"Rape and murder. And we're wasting time."

When I left fifty-three minutes later, I had photographed what I needed.

Randy looked like he could wait another decade or so before our next meeting.

ఆ

Stretching out on the grass in Central Park, I read my photos of the manual and developed a quick loathing for all car salesmen everywhere.

CHAPTER 25.

Manhattan still had some party stores that sold costumes. Most huddled near Times Square where porn stars and tourists could buy Richard Nixon masks and sex toys at the same counter. Maybe it spiced up their visit to the Big Apple, home of sin and depravity.

On Ninth Avenue and 44th Street, the bored Asian beauty behind the counter sold me a glue-on moustache to match my hair. A pair of thick black eyeglasses completed the total geek look.

My shoes turned west onto 46th Street. New York Central Railroad tracks ran through the a cleft cut through the gray schist. Above the tracks, the Salvation Army Thrift heaven Sharing-Is-Caring store sold me a summer-weight suit the color of tea. A forgettable white shirt and obligatory tie followed.

A shopping cart on Tenth Avenue sold me a polyester fedora hat, with a frivolous feather spouting from the band.

More front-page color pictures of the raped and murdered Ms. Tracy Lowell, age 44, from *The Post* decorated newsstands along my walk. TV store windows were filled with broadcast images of detectives in baggy suits looking somber around her brownstone.

☙

I trudged back to Leo's garage, brown-bagging my shopping treasures. He watched me put a pebble inside my shoe.

"What crazy stuff you doing now?" Leo asked.

"The old-fashioned Pinkerton sleuth, master of disguise," I said. "Smiting the wicked in for truth and justice."

"Why you put *el guijo* in your shoe?"

"So I won't have to remember to limp," I said. "The pebble will remind me."

"So why?"

"Limping changes my look. Officer Max does not limp. But this new person, who looks different, limps. And Playpenners look away from a person who walks with difficulty like that. Because they are fit and spry and healthy."

Changing into my new suit, I recalled cop stories that dead men's families sometimes supplied these clothes to thrift shops. Most cops refused to buy second-hand clothes.

☙

Heat from the sidewalk seemed to rise up and cook me in this suit. Its material did not breathe.

I made it to East 83rd Street.

By now, the block felt like home. The tiny surviving shops for shoe repair, dry cleaning, fortune telling and newspapers calmed me.

Threading my way to Youth At Play, I tried to look innocent and dull. If beatniks saw through my disguise, it would set ComPol back twenty years.

Inside the store, the same woman looked up from her counter as I entered. A beer smell soured the air. 1010 WINS All News radio hammered away in the background.

Lessons from the salesman's manual swam back to me.

"Good afternoon, ma'am," I said. "My name is Robert Kremser and I'm trying to locate a woman who had worked here. She has come into some money."

My speech slowed into a country rhythm. It was a ploy to make me sound different from Officer Max on the beat.

She stirred behind the counter and made a face.

"Someone who worked here?" she asked.

"Yes. And the attorney has been trying to locate the heirs to this inheritance. Or else, it goes into escrow. We are authorized to pay a percentage to anyone who helps us locate her."

She leaned a bit closer over the counter.

"What's that?" she asked.

"We can pay. For information."

"Why did you come here?"

Her voice sounded less like a city accent. When she said 'what,' the 'a' tone sounded like someone from upstate New York.

"Because we were told that this woman, the heiress, had worked here, in the summer of 1967, as a teenager. It may have been part-time."

"That's not just yesterday," she said.

"Were you the owner then?"

"I rent here."

"It's a great location," I said, to keep her talking. "The Upper East Side. Clean, safe and famous."

This was another trick from the used-car whores of America.

She smirked.

This store was a stagnant backwater in the Playpen and she knew it.

"How much money can you pay out?" she asked. "Is that legal?"

"Ten percent of the total. And, yes, it's all legal. It's arranged for and stipulated in the will."

The store told me nothing new. But I looked past her thin frame through a doorway, I could make out a cot in the gloom in the back room. A magazine lay next to the cot, on the floor.

"How much is the estate?" she asked.

"Ethically, that is private info. But, use your own judgment. Do you think that the family lawyer would contract me for a small sum? We're talking lots of pictures of dead presidents here. How long have you rented this space?"

"17 years."

"And who owned it before then?"

"Some Hunky."

"Excuse me?"

"A Hungarian guy."

"I see. What building does he live in now?"

"Some building in Hungary. He went back home."

"I see," I said.

Stepping closer to the doorway, I tried to look into the cot room.

"Here is my card," I said. "Oh, I want to make sure that I give you the right one. Let me get better light."

I zigzagged near the counter.

"I left my reading glasses at home," I said.

"Hey, you can't go back there."

The magazine near the cot was called *Killing Fighting*. On the cover, in splashy colors, two hairy, bearded brutes pummeled each other.

Never heard of it.

I stepped back towards her.

"I was just trying to get better light to see," I said. "That's all."

The card was a pre-fabricated job. It had my fake name and a disposable cellphone number printed on it. The words "Inheritance Recovery Professional" underneath made me look like someone scrambling to turn a buck.

"I don't know her," she said.

"Who?"

"Whoever worked here," she said. "Whatever you said."

My side-step to the doorway had been a mistake. She was getting suspicious.

CHAPTER 26.

I could see a wet spot forming from fear-sweat under my shirt front. This was taxing me. It would be droll if my first heart attack felled me right here.

Lieutenant Hundshamer of CRIT could pluck me right off the ambulance.

"Her name was Amelia Novak," I said.

She shook her head.

"After she worked here, her mother married a Mr. Charles Drake," I said. "He was an advertising man who did very well indeed with money. When he died, that money passed to his wife, of course. Then the wife, Mrs. Evelyn Novak Drake, left all the estate to her daughter Amelia. Now, you can pick up some of it, just for helping us find Amelia."

She shook her head.

"I don't know," she said. "I've got some work to do here."

We both knew that was a lie.

"Where can I reach the current owner?" I asked.

The salesman's manual would be proud of me.

"Don't know," she said.

That chalked up another lie.

"How is that possible?" I asked.

We were word-dueling now and we both knew it.

"Leave your card," she said. "I'll ask him to call you."

"Actually, that was exactly what I hoped that you would say," I said, treading water and trying to buy time. "Would you mind speaking on the phone with the attorney handling the estate?"

She shrugged. Her dress slipped, showing mealy and scarred skin.

"All this can translate into a finder's fee for you," I said. "That is a percentage of the final estate. Mr. Drake spent his last years in the Turks and Caicos Islands, and we are operating under their inheritance laws, not New York's."

Let her try to check on inheritance laws on American citizens living in the Turks and Caicos Islands. She would have to travel there to research it. I knew because I had tried.

"Well, I have taken enough of your time," I said. Again, nerves had pushed my voice higher. "Do you have a card where I may contact you?"

"Nope."

"What is your telephone number here?"

"I'll call you –"

"But our attorney," I broke in. "Remember, there is some money in this for you."

"I don't like giving out the number."

"Well, that is a problem. So, you want me to come back to deliver any message?"

She told me her number. I scribbled it on the back of the fake business card. My palm was wet.

"Don't be calling me all the time or anything."

Nobody would want to, I thought. This is the most depressing toy store that I had ever seen. No parent who liked his own child would ever return here. How she stayed afloat here formed its own mystery.

"Good day," I said. "And thank you so much. You know my name is Kremser. But what is yours, please?"

"Jesus, you want everything."

"So that we can make out a check for your help."

"I'm Mrs. Swifty. And I've got work to do now."

Stepping back up the steps and onto the street was a relief.

My beatniks still dangled along the street.

The same mix of tenements and yuppie high-rises showed their fronts.

Everyone seemed to stare at the limping man with glasses and a moustache under his fedora hat.

As I passed by Kimbry's apartment building, I heard his same hoarse voice again.

"You think you're going to disrespect me like that?" he shouted. "I'll knock you around the block just for exercise."

The other beatniks heard this through the open window. They acted as if it was nothing new.

"And don't give me that look in the back of my head!" he went on.

By training, my shoes turned towards the shouting. Cops would always try to settle down a voice like that, with violence in it about to erupt.

Everything in me wanted to step in now.

But I could not move Kimbry around the way that he needed. It would blow today's hustle and maybe my whole routine.

ꟹ

To cover myself and my little fairy tale, I went into the other shops and asked about the fake Amelia Novak.

By now, my lies about old Amelia were starting to feel natural. Maybe all car dealers felt this way.

My beatniks in the stores were too busy to talk about much. They had acted differently to Max, the cop in uniform, paying me fake respect. That showed me again that ComPol did not work.

"But I got something good," I told Jody over the cell.

"Mrs. Swifty gave me her name. And that Killing Fighting magazine on the floor near the cot is not bedtime reading material for most women. That means that some man stays there sometimes. And he may be her son. He might just be the Horn Bug."

CHAPTER 27.

Saving some part of the day, I trudged back to Leo's garage and changed into my T-shirt, blue jeans and sneakers again. It soothed me after that unbreathing plastic business suit.

I went back to Information Services and startled the bright young actress-hopeful, this month starring as the company receptionist.

Maybe they were not expecting any more customers today.

With the air of one dispensing alms, she passed me the report marked "Secret and Confidential."

I read it, shook my head and asked for the executive who had taken my payment.

Black Irish, with a heavy five o'clock shadow and unblinking blue eyes behind serious glasses, Mr. Tom Wickham unfolded his black summer suit to usher me into his office.

His manner said that we were going to discuss Serious Matters like Adults. Hot-diggity.

"This report says that the owner of the toy store, Youth At Play, is a Friedrich Poryitko, now living in Poland," I observed. "Can we get any better data than that?"

"Well, that's pretty useful info," Wickham said. "You can get a fact-finder operating in Poland through the Internet."

"Oh, really?" I asked. His office smelled of Old Spice cologne and his own wet-doggy scent. "You're sure that Brother Friedrich, the owner, is in Poland?"

"Rock-sure."

"How about Hungary?" I asked.

"Now, why would you ask that?"

"Because I found out something on my own."

"You were advised not to approach them without checking with us first," Wickham said. "You paid top dollar for a top-level job."

"I'll agree with the first half of that sentence," I said.

He gave me the same look that many others had given.

"Well," he breathed out.

"Do you have any affiliate that you can recommend in Poland?"

"Of course."

"And they'll be glad to help me," I said. "For a fee."

He nodded like a professional, pained and noncommittal.

"What's the name of the woman working in the store now?" I asked.

He unkinked himself a bit more.

"This is only a preliminary report," he said. "We could re-evaluate for another report."

"Do you know her name?" I asked. "Simple 'yes' or naked 'no'."

"Not at this time."

"Any ink-stained wretch available in Hungary to check on the owner for me?" I asked.

"We have affiliate researchers throughout Europe."

My chest heaved in and out. Something inside me was getting close to a revelation.

"I don't know much about business," I said. "Never did and probably never will. But I've had a front-row seat on incompetence. And padded bills."

"There's no point in discussing this further," he said. "I'm sorry that you appear dissatisfied with our service."

He and his business suit stood up.

"Her name is Swifty," I said. "And the store owner is in Hungary. Not Poland. That's what I found out on my own."

"It may be untrue."

"Why should she lie? There's no money in it for her. Unlike some that I could name."

"I think that you're being unprofessional about this."

"Oh, that word," I said. "Maybe I can improve. As I ask for a refund on my money."

"Why would you feel that way?"

"Because I'm getting the story of Goliath and the Lion from your outfit," I said.

"Our company policy is not to entertain ideas for refunds. We can renegotiate another contract and apply what you have spent to a credit."

Then it was time for me to stand up and go. My left hand clenched. It would feel good to start throwing hooks with it.

One would double Mr. Tom Wickham up inside his spiffy sucker-swindling costume.

"I'm thinking about legal action," I said.

"That might open up difficulties," he said. "We ran a brief credit check on you when we took this assignment."

"Hope you didn't overcharge yourselves."

"Your employment came up. Why would a policeman pay for this kind of research? Perhaps there is something that could embarrass you, during the discovery phase in a civil trial."

"Your type never understands my type," I said. "My kind of legal action is standing in front of your office, holding a large banner describing the great and low-priced work that your firm does."

"That sounds pretty juvenile."

"Public street, public expression and you can't shut me up without going into court yourself," I said. "Talks like this make me believe in the street and nothing but the street more and more."

CHAPTER 28.

"Today's my day for professionals," I told Dr. Markwall, my friendly neighborhood psychiatrist, on the phone. "I think that my subject has a mother sheltering and protecting him. Why don't you cheer me up with something that I can use?"

"I could throw some jargon at you about what we call 'Helicopter Parenting,'" he said. "That is when a parent hovers over a child constantly, ready to swoop down and save them."

"This is my subject, the Horn Bug, that you're talking about?" I asked.

"Yes. But this is just my theory, Max. From reading up on sex killers and looking at this current case, I can make some educated guesses. A parent who over-protects a child is setting that same child up for being unable to handle life's problems as an adult. That same child, under certain conditions and stressors, may show anger towards adults of the same gender as the overprotecting parent."

"This sounds pretty shaky," I said.

"It has to be, until we can interview him as a patient. But your subject is much more violent than we could expect from just being overprotected. We don't know why, do we?"

"Not yet."

"By being overprotective, the mother has perverted the norm. The baseline of care is flawed. So he will reciprocate. He will have to overcompensate for what she has done."

"You're losing me, Doctor. How will he overcompensate?"

"Simple. He will overprotect his own mother. Where other better-adjusted adults will let the parent fend for themselves, this one will go overboard. He will do anything to ward off reality from his mother."

"I wish that someone would keep reality away from me," I said.

ɞ

Manhattan seemed to press down on me today.

Oily clouds roved restlessly overhead. Away from the sun, the city cooled.

I called Nancy, the fighting professional beauty, who had taught me how to stay alive so far.

"Nancy, what can you tell me about the magazine *Killing Fighting*?" I asked.

"That's hard-core. Only real serious characters read that rag. Most of us call that magazine 'irresponsible' and 'maniacal' and cute stuff like that."

"Why?"

"Because they teach everything possible, just to damage and cripple. They don't care a hang for gradual escalation of force. They justify deadly force if someone makes you nervous. I don't know how they stay in business."

"So they are bad rascals?"

"If someone who reads that garbage comes at you, bury him," she said. "That's my only advice. Nothing else will work."

ɞ

I hustled back onto the subway towards Jody's home.

Romantic that she was, she was having a locksmith cut me a spare key for her front door sometime today. I could come and go like a real adult whenever I wanted.

She would finish her last class at nine tonight. We could dine at the Jamaican restaurant near St. Nicholas Avenue. Their menu boasted salt ackee and turtle soup, the real thing, not mock.

ɞ

I came up out of the subway at 135th Street and headed north for her brownstone.

My ankle ached again.

Behind me, a car door opened. I turned my head. Lieutenant Lenny was stepping out of the car.

I sprinted.

"Royster!" he shouted. "You Funny Bunny!"

"Like old times," I said.

My feet pounded the sidewalk. I could not last long.

"Stop! Police!"

"We going official now."

The car engine caught and roared. His siren blared.

I reached the end of the block and went right.

His car barreled after me.

I stopped and ran back the way I had come.

He was already past me. His brakes squealed.

That was something that I could outrace him on. On foot, I could reverse directions. Other cars would block him from doing so.

Lenny was working alone. CRIT usually did. They never trusted other cops to support them.

He backed up after me now.

The radio gurgled in his car.

My feet headed for Saint Nicholas Park.

Before he could get uniforms to grab me, I might be able to hide in the park.

Another siren whooped nearby.

A second siren joined in shrieking harmony.

Sidewalkers stopped to look at me.

"The white po-lice chasing whites in Harlem now!" someone shouted. "That's what happens when you in-teg-rate a neighborhood."

"Sociology," I said, vaulting across the avenue.

A blue-and-white roared down the avenue after me. Angry engine noise buzzsawed.

I leaped up the steps past the subway entrance.

The park opened before me, green and lush and inviting.

More NYPD cars thundered in, from every direction.

A helicopter dipped down.

I dove inside the first grove of trees and lay there, panting and cursing and hacking up phlegm.

☙

Lying in the park, I could feel my heart pounding against the dirt.

NYPD cops did not like to cordon off a park and search for someone. Doing that always caused some citizens to panic. They were convinced that their baby was playing in that park.

More importantly, New Yorkers in general never obeyed cops anyway. They would not leave parks whenever the cops told them to. They would ignore them profanely.

So the park would stay open.

Blue-and-whites kept bouncing past my hiding place in the bushes. I saw them through a gap in the foliage.

The helicopter kept chopping up the sky with noise.

The helicopters and patrol cars circled back and forth, pinwheeling and banking in a weird three-dimensional law enforcement ballet. It looked like a great free life, the kind I was about to lose. My world would be locked down in gray metal rooms in Bellevue.

One car parked near me, watching. I could hear their radio.

"Be advised. Suspect is a male white, about 50 years old, red over green," the radio said. "Six feet one, 230 pounds."

Hundshamer was making me older and fatter. He was my pal.

"Former Member-of-the-Service, possibly armed," the radio said.

Knowing my Patrol pals, I was hoping that they would drift out of the park as soon as a sergeant turned his back. They would lay low near a friendly pizzeria and replenish their precious body needs.

Nobody wanted to catch an ex-cop. Nobody wanted to do anything for CRIT.

Hundshamer's blue Monte Carlo swung back along my pathway. Then he stopped.

He sensed that I could not have gotten very far. Both he and I had chased enough clients to have a sense of how far they could run.

The smart ones did what I had done. They went to ground right away and froze. Movement would give them away.

Time was on my side. The cops would have to answer other radio calls. The bosses would not authorize overtime on something like this. So Hundshamer would have to move fast and on his own.

That was like what I had to do.

He hunched out of his car. His step showed an old knee injury on his left. He moved like my old Uncle Eddy after falling down a flight of subway stairs.

The scarred and bruised hand gripped his suit jacket, the one the other cop had torn apart with his teeth.

He drew his service gun and held it down his side.

That meant serious business. The Job drilled and trained all of us never to draw unless absolutely necessary. So Hundshamer had a strong idea that I was nearby.

He moved quietly, despite his bad knee. The sunlight made him look older and more frail than before. Veins showed in his neck and forehead. He swallowed hard. His eyes bulged.

"Hey, Lieu!" the driver of another patrol car shouted. The car bounced down the pathway. "Are you nuts, walking point by yourself? This guy's a cuckoo, right? Don't do that."

"It's way too dangerous," his partner added.

"This guy's supposed to be carrying, right? Don't play it this way, on your own."

"Yeah, we'll check for you," the partner said. "Just stay put, Lieu."

They slopped out of their car and towards my hiding place.

"I'll take a look-see," the driver said. He was a beefy black cop with long flared sideburns, mirror sunglasses and a big round beer gut. "Three is safer."

He stepped closer.

I froze.

"Fuck CRIT," he said softly.

Nobody else could hear him.

Maybe he was just chanting the Patrol mantra.

Or maybe he had seen me and was reassuring me.

The brotherhood of cops still amazed me. They would not want to be the one to arrest another cop, even for murder. They would leave that for the hated ones, like Hundshamer.

"Nobody anywhere around here, Lieu," he hollered. "Let's keep looking."

Hundshamer shook his head and came closer.

The black cop looked at Hundshamer's scarred hand. With his time on the Job, he probably knew the story of that hand.

"Hey, Lieu, you okay?" the other cop said. With a huge belly and slow thoughtful moves, he looked like what we cops called 'a hair bag.' A hair bag did nothing unless he had to and waited for that 20-year pension.

"You look a bit shaky," he went on. "You want to sit down for a bit?"

"I'm okay," Hundshamer said.

"No, really, Lieu," he said. "This hump ain't worth getting a coronary over."

Hundshamer knew that any cop over 50 was scrutinized and checked for heart trouble. If he showed any signs now, the brass would take him off the street. So he had to get away from these two nursemaid types.

"I'm good to go," Hundshamer said.

He limped back to his car, got in and drove away. You could tell that he was wired up about it.

"What's his problem?" the Hair Bag asked.

"They only put the screwiest ones in CRIT. Especially the lieutenants."

The cops slouched back to their car, settled back into it like two hippos getting into hot water and drove away.

I sank down in my hiding place.

The radio sounds vanished.

The helicopter soared away.

Still, I stayed frozen in my eight-foot piece of Manhattan.

Kids came back, playing and hooting around.

It felt good after the copper merry-go-round.

Salsa music came from radios.

You could tell that the cops had left. Marijuana smells flowered nearby.

I dozed. The adrenaline did that sometimes.

Darkness came.

CHAPTER 29.

I phoned Jody from the bushes.

"Don't tell me anything!" she said. "That lieutenant said that he'll arrest me."

I heaved out a breath.

"For talking on the phone?" I asked. "They generally don't land on you too hard for that."

"Do you always have to wisecrack?"

"Seems like."

"I am done with you!"

"If that happens, then we both lose. Is anyone watching your place now?"

"Yes. He was watching my house when you came. My house! Like I was a criminal. What did I do?"

"Let's talk in person," I said.

"Are you deranged? I never want to see you again."

"Meet me at the Harlem 125th Street Metro-North Station in an hour. In the waiting room."

"I can't do that. They'll follow me there and arrest you."

"Not me. Just watch for me."

Emerging from the bushes that had been my nest, I scanned the park for cops. Nobody looked suspicious.

Hustling down to the train station at 125th Street, I kept watching for a CRIT tail team. I double-backed and went down one-way streets and did a few other tricks from paperback mysteries.

Dry-cleaning always took time.

Jody showed, looking slimmer and younger and frightened in a peach-colored sash dress. It showed her suntanned strong back muscles. The air of patchouli rose from her.

"You look lovely," I said. "Worth going to the asylum for."

"Stop it, Max. I don't like to think about that happening to you. That lieutenant, he frightened me."

"Think about that," I said. "Right now, in his view, you're the lover of a murder suspect. If I get clear by catching the Horn Bug, then you're a faithful friend and companion. Nothing adverse there."

"He threatened to get me fired."

"Do you think that City College will fire a teacher because some hairy-legged police lieutenant tells them to?"

"I'll lose my sabbatical."

"Don't do that!" I said.

She stepped back.

"I never heard that voice from you before," she said.

"On Patrol, a black cloud follows you and every day, it gets closer," I said.

"You're talking in riddles?"

"Hundshamer was a conscientious cop years ago. But a cop crippled his hand. And now he exists to make cops think that they are caught up in that black cloud. Don't let him pull you into it."

"But he is so composed."

"That's his craft, Jody. He fools cops into thinking that there is no way out. Then the cop pleads guilty or resigns or flees. Sometimes he or she does The Honorable Thing."

"What is 'the Honorable Thing?'"

"Suicide."

"I can't believe that."

"Because you and the other civilians never know. There exists a war in the shadows between street cops and CRIT. And the Knapp and the Mollen Commissions, Citizens' Crime Commission and all the ladies garden clubs who slam the cops. The only ones who know this are cops. Or those who fall in love with cops."

She hung her head.

"So," I breathed. It rocked my frame.

Commuters roved past us, munching takeout French fries.

"Tomorrow, meet me at six at East 83rd Street and First Avenue," I said.

Then I told her how to look and what to wear.

"That's twisted behavior," she said. "It won't work."

"It's our only chance."

"And what will you be wearing?"

"Me?" I said. "That's easy. I'll be in uniform."

CHAPTER 30.

"Good morning," Nancy said.

In the background, someone walloped a heavy bag.

"I've got news for you," she murmured in her bedroom voice. "In my underground world, I squeezed some old friends."

"I'll bet that you did."

"They reminded me about your screwball. I had forgotten him. Too many drugs, I guess. The one that you're hunting is a long tall drink of water, blond crew cut, and he wanted lessons. I saw him spar and rejected him. He did not want to learn. He loved to hurt."

"Name, Nancy. What's his name?"

"He uses fighting names, different ones. Odin, Charlemagne or Custer. All five Armed Forces rejected him because he is a cuckoo. So he calls himself a soldier of fortune. He haunts the city and hurts women."

"Can anyone find him?"

"If more of you cops ever cared about women, he would be doing state prison time," she said. "But he knows how to hurt women who don't matter."

"Like who?"

"Welfare mamas with troubles."

"Yeah," I said. "So tell me who cares about them? And how much?"

"Depressing."

"Thank you, my dear. I'll protect you and your honey-bunch. Please keep pressing for a name."

"Thank you, my dear. I'll help you and your honey-bunch. Please keep pressing for a name."

My palms wetted again.

I called Lipkin's cell and gave him what I had.

"Didn't I tell you that CRIT has this case?" Lipkin snapped. "I can't do anything but wiggle my eyebrows. Or get fired for insubordination."

"Can you get me an anti-crime team tonight in Manhattan?"

"Don't ask me that. I'll hang up right now."

"Al –"

Lipkin ended the call; the background noise snapping immediately to silence.

☙

On Second Avenue, I shopped in the Stuyvesant Square Thrift shop, bought some women's clothes and bagged them.

Then I slunk to Leo's garage and switched into a fresh uniform. The shotgun fitted back into the surgical band under my thigh. Breaking it again, I checked the red plastic shells. Combat jitters made me keep checking.

Four extra rounds went into my left front pocket.

Then I sallied forth, hopefully for the last time.

☙

Clouds rolled by with sticky heat above East 83rd Street.

The brickwork mixed with colorful painted storefronts.

The street door to Kimbry's building was locked.

A woman hung in the hallway, checking her mailbox.

My knuckles rapped the street door's window.

"Excuse me," I said. "Police. Me, Max."

She saw my uniform and nodded.

"Can you please open this door?"

She shook her head and stepped upstairs.

"Thank you, ComPol," I said aloud. "Thank you very much indeed."

I leaned left and rapped on Kimbry's window.

Kimbry came to the window, looking truculent.

"You," he said. "I went to Internal Affairs and complained on you. They gave me a card with a number to call. They're after you."

"Yup. Can you open the door?"

"Why should I?"

"Figure it out. I'm getting in sooner or later. Then you and I are going to dance. Right now, you decide if you want a happy dance or an angry one."

He made a face and turned away.

I slipped out my ASP folding baton and whipped it open. The tip tapped against the window glass.

Kimbry stopped.

The tip kept tapping.

The tapping got louder.

He threw up his thick hands and nodded.

I stopped the baton.

He came out into the hallway and half-opened the street door. I put my foot into the doorway.

"You're not supposed to use your stick with that," he said. "That's another charge against you."

His daughter appeared behind him in the hall.

"Thalia, my dear," I said. "Did you get a restraining order against your Dad here? Remember, you said that you would."

She went back into her apartment and clicked the door.

"A daughter can't get a restraining order against her father," Kimbry said.

"How wrong you are," I said. "Even if they live together, she can get one. And I think that she did get one. She is just not talking about it."

"Nothing you can do," Kimbry said.

"Yes, I can. You've got ten minutes to pack your trash and get out of here."

"You can't do that. It's against the law."

"I don't think so," I said. "If it is, why don't you try calling 911 right now? And when the sergeant gets here, we'll check your daughter for recent bruises. Maybe have a sex counselor talk to her."

"I'm not leaving," he said. "I got the card."

He reached into his pocket.

My hand closed on his wrist and pulled it out of his pocket. He was holding his wallet, half-open. It fell to the floor. Cards spread out on the floor. He reached for them but I pushed my leg against his arm, pinning it to the wall.

"Looky here," I said. "A Visa card. Yours?"

"You can't search me!"

"I didn't. You reached in your pocket and I'm defending myself against a possible attack. There's a woman's name on that card. Is that card maybe stolen, Kimbry? Lot of mysterious charges on it?"

"You can't do this!"

"Nine minutes."

I bore Kimbry into the apartment and went to his closet. He packed his all-time favorite clothes into a woman's cloth carpet-bag style suitcase.

"You're gone now or else I bust you for that woman's credit card," I said. "Receiving stolen property."

I walked him and his bulging carpet-bag down the steps and into the street. My beatniks watched.

"Officer, you can't throw him out," one said.

"My friend is leaving voluntarily," I said. "Before he becomes a client."

"That's just not right," another beatnik said.

"ComPol, ComPol," I sang under my breath. "What makes your big head so hard?"

"You'll be working night security at Toys 'R' Us," Kimbry said.

"With union benefits?" I asked.

Kimbry waddled towards Second Avenue, the carpet-bag banging against his legs.

A crowd had meshed together to watch him.

Their faces did not look friendly.

CHAPTER 31.

The rain clouds rolled in closer.

Air changed and grew gummy thick.

Trying to walk off the adrenaline dump from Kimbry, I paced the block.

Nobody was talking to me.

Jody showed up, walking from First Avenue. She looked angry and abused. Her body seemed to writhe inside the old clothes that she wore. I had asked her to wear them tonight.

I brought her into a service walkway behind 358 East 83rd Street. Garbage smell covered us. The plastic bag from my shopping was still wadded up there.

"Please, hold still," I said. "Think of this as a play. Underground theater."

My fingers mussed up her hair. The thick blonde tresses hung limply. Bright red lipstick made her look like a child's toy doll. I painted two lipstick marks on her cheeks and thumbed dirty band-aids along her high cheekbones.

The loud green blouse from the thrift shop went over her head. My fingers ripped the neck of the shirt and let it lay.

I tore a T-shirt into strips and tied them around her legs.

The strips hung.

"I look really crazy now, Max," she said.

"It'll all be over soon," I said. "One way or another."

Putting more Band-Aids across the backs of her hands helped the image. I tore tinfoil from a roll and stuck bits of it into the T-shirt strips around her legs.

"Now you're protected against the radiation," I said. "Don't you feel better? The others all do."

Now Jody looked like a wild woman.

I reached in the same bag and took out a six-dollar plastic rain poncho from Duane Reade Drugstores. It was huge, 3XL, dark green and lightweight, for New York's summers. I put it on over my uniform. It covered me up.

Nobody could tell that I was in uniform now.

I took off my uniform hat and put it inside the same plastic bag. For a hat, I took out a big green cotton slouch hat. It drooped down over my forehead.

"You look way different now," she said. "Nobody will recognize you in that get-up."

"Same to you, Professor."

Jody left me.

She must have taken acting classes because she went straight into Method-Acted homeless psycho.

Her hands moved. Her voice croaked.

On the back of her blouse, I had printed in purple Magic Marker:

> No family can employ more than three
> servants. If you do not work for my
> family, please do not hit me.

She cawed like one of the three witches from Macbeth's opening scene.

A finger went into her nostril and dug.

Beatniks walking down the street avoided her.

From my hiding place, I watched her.

She stepped down into Youth At Play and entered the store.

Shouts came forth.

Jody came back out of the store, waving her arms.

She stomped her foot and walked away.

Then she walked up the block and then came back.

She went down into the store again.

Rain started hitting the streets.

Beatniks went inside.

Some watched her from their windows.

Jody came back outside.

In my disguise, I walked past the store and looked in.

Mrs. Swifty stood behind her counter.

Jody stomped around the store.

Then Jody came back out.

She rolled her head in front of the store.

Hidden back in the service area, I shucked off my disguise.

Jody wobbled away from the store.

Back in uniform, I stepped back outside on the street.

The beatniks saw me and motioned to Jody.

I walked up to the corner.

A blue-and-white NYPD car rolled up 83rd Street. The cops inside were strangers to me.

Feeling panic tear at me, I flagged them down.

"Yo, guy?" the black woman driving asked me.

"I got this nut job," I said. "I'll deal with her, okay."

"We got a radio run," she said.

I stepped closer to her.

Maybe they would see that my shield was a phony.

"Guys, spread the word," I said. "CRIT is setting up any cop who responds to this block. Stay away. Don't respond to this nut lady job."

"I can't hear you, Officer," the driver said. "Not one word."

She gunned the car away.

Jody swung back to the store and waved her arms.

I went back to my hidey-hole and put on my poncho and hat again. My fingers tapped the shotgun under my leg.

Rain came down and stopped.

The whole city waited.

Jody went in front of the store and yanked on the doorknob.

Mrs. Swifty had locked it.
I waited across the street, hidden in a doorway.
Jody stayed in front of the store, waving her hands again.
Then a man stepped out from another doorway.
He walked towards her.
I had seen him before.
It was the Horn Bug.

CHAPTER 32.

The Horn Bug walked towards Jody.

I stepped as close as I could.

My hands shook again.

They flip-flopped as I bent down and yanked the shotgun from under my pants leg.

The Horn Bug swiveled, saw my uniform and kicked backwards.

His foot slammed into the shotgun.

POW-WAH!

My shotgun exploded.

The roar filled the block.

Beatniks froze on the sidewalk. Up above, heads came out of windows.

My shotgun skittered across the sidewalk and into the gutter.

He kicked again. His foot caught my thigh. I felt the muscles behind his kick.

My leg died. I flopped down.

"Police officer!" I croaked. I rolled over and fumbled out the ASP baton.

He pirouetted.

I swung the baton at his kneecap. But he was already leaping away.

Then he danced back. He stomped my left foot. Something cracked inside me. I could feel it. More pain corkscrewed my head.

The baton caught his thigh.

It did not stop him.

Rain came down. It fell harder this time.

Rolling back, I dodged his kicks.

One kick caught my head.

The hot asphalt cooled from the rain.

My own sweat mixed with the uniform smell.

The Horn Bug looked bigger than I remembered him. Maybe the boy was still getting his full growth.

His forearms bulged. Muscles rippled under his green camouflage T-shirt.

Eyes slitted in his All-American face.

I kept rolling.

Then I pushed up from the concrete.

My left ankle screamed again.

I dropped back down.

He had broken my ankle. I could not stand.

He whirled back in again and kicked my hand holding the baton.

The baton pinwheeled away. It hit a car windshield.

The windshield shattered. The car's alarm blared.

Jody hurled herself down the block.

"Call 911!" she shouted. "He's a killer!"

Beatniks stabbed their cellphones.

Lila scrambled out of the coffee shop.

A baseball bat waved in her hands.

The Horn Bug turned back and kicked at me.

Nancy had taught me how to block this. My leg flew out and caught his shin.

Jody threw a punch that caught his head. It stopped him.

Then the Horn Bug threw out an elbow sideways. It caught Jody's belly. His fist flew downwards and hit below her belt.

She crumpled.

The fist flung up in the same motion.

It hit her jaw.

It was a wicked three-in-one punch. It would destroy me.

Jody went back. Blood spurted from her face. She weaved and dropped down on the sidewalk. Her head hit the concrete with a THOCK!

"Help me!" I rasped. My voice choked. "My beatniks!"

The Horn Bug kicked again.

I blocked it with my right foot. It stung my whole body.

My beatniks came closer.

They started forming around him, keeping back.

"I'll kill every one of you!" he shouted. "Army Special Forces! HOO-RAH!"

"He's a bed-wetter!" I shouted. "No Army. You beatniks can take him."

One of the beatniks threw a punch to his face. It was Eddie, my beer-drinking buddy.

The Horn Bug bent down. His hands and elbows flew. They hit Eddie's neck and temple.

Eddie dropped to the sidewalk.

The Horn Bug simpered.

He was enjoying this.

"He killed him!" a man's throaty voice called.

The beatniks moved back.

"No, he didn't!" I shouted. "Eddie's still moving-"

A foot kicked my gut. My wind blew out. I could not speak.

The Horn Bug kicked at me again. This time, I rolled to one side.

My breath rasped out. Words whistled in my throat.

He was silencing me.

Nerves made me retch dry heaves.

Playing for time, I rolled sideways.

My voice strained to come back.

"Listen, beatniks!" I said. "He killed two women in the neighborhood here. You're the only chance to stop him."

A wooden crutch came down and splintered on the Horn Bug's head. He shook it off. A chunky Latina woman, black ponytail flying, hit him in the ribs with a bent golf club.

Mama Swifty kept squinting at us, hunched outside her store.

I rolled over onto my gut. That gave my back to him.

He could not resist it.

Nancy had taught me this mule kick.

I flattened my palms on the sidewalk, pushed up and kicked backwards like a mule.

He caught my foot and ripped it backwards. Ligaments tore. I screamed with pain. I was paralyzed. But he was tied up, holding my foot. He needed to hold onto it. That froze him.

A blue-and-white cop car turned in from First Avenue.

The red-and-white roof light spun.

The Horn Bug froze.

He dropped his hands.

I could barely see the cop driving. The cop scanned the block. The parked cars blocked him from seeing me.

Probably the call had gone out as "Fistfight. No weapons involved."

"Over here!" some man shouted.

"He's killing this cop!" Lila shouted.

"I hope not," I whispered.

Another NYPD car rolled alongside the first.

Maybe the cops were passing the word on the CRIT rumor that I had planted.

Lila waved the bat.

They rocketed past us.

"They're going away!" Lila screamed.

"They didn't see us!" some man shouted.

"Saw enough," I panted. "Saw a CRIT set-up. I've outsmarted myself."

At the corner, they cruised. I knew the routine. They were just putting on a show in case anyone important was watching. Hairbags did it all the time. It became second nature.

"I won't let them put me back into that hospital," the Horn Bug said.

"Gotcha," I said.

"Staff raped me.," he said. "They buttered this blond boy. Officer, I'm going to cripple you. Pain all the time."

"I got that already," I said.

"Funny man, huh? I been watching you from the rooftop, horsing around here on the street. Messing with my mom."

"Beatniks!" I shouted. "Don't let him run!"

The beatniks stepped closer.

They looked like Early Man trying to encircle a wild beast.

"ComPol!" I hissed.

The Horn Bug kicked again. A beatnik dropped. Another ran.

But another tackled the Horn Bug and pulled him back down. He swung a carpet-bag suitcase that hit the Horn Bug's head.

It was Kimbry swinging that carpet-bag.

Someone else poked a broom, wooden end first. The Horn Bug caught the wood, tore it loose from them and threw it down.

Some beatniks ran.

Others lunged at him and onto his back. He struck out. Their body weight pulled him down to the sidewalk.

"We got him!" Lila shouted.

"All for Max!" someone else hollered.

"Beatniks, for Max!" Lila said.

Beer guts and varicose veins flopped onto the Horn Bug.

My fingers unsnapped the cuff case.

The bodies rolled onto me.

Smells of beer, sweat and grass choked me. The handcuffs came out.

The Horn Bug saw the cuffs. He rolled his body on top of my hand holding the cuffs. I could not move it. He ground my knuckles into the pavement.

My hand went numb. The fingers opened.

The cheers stopped.

We all rolled more.

"He's getting up!"

The Horn Bug reared up, hitting a beatnik across the throat.

I lunged and grabbed his ankles. He tried kicking. I put my steak-and-whiskey body against the ankles and heaved.

He spilled down again.

"Beatniks, for Max!"

My gunbelt held another cuff case. I stretched back my arm, unsnapped the case and came out with the cuffs.

He flailed.

My hands grabbed his arm. I bent the arm into a jujitsu lock.

He smirked.

"Bullshit!" he said.

He straightened out his arm and slithered out of the lock.

Nancy the mayhem teacher's words echoed back to me.

"You need to practice those locks all the time for them to work," Nancy had said.

I reared up to gain distance. My elbow swung into his face. I could feel my skin split open on his teeth.

Twice more, I struck.

He gasped and dropped back.

With my left, I swung the cuffs over my head and brought one down against his wrist. The metal hit the bone and the cuff spun around, locking his wrist.

He head-butted me.

Skyrockets burst my eyes.

Blind, I fell back against a parked car.

My eyes blurred.

I gripped his free arm and speared it with the open cuff. It clicked shut.

He tried getting up.

Jody slammed him back down.

Her green eyes burned.

I fell on top of him, gasping.

Someone's sneaker kicked his forehead. It smudged his skin.

"Beatniks, we took him for Max!"

"Sure did," I breathed. "That's real Community Policing."

Blue-and-whites roared onto the block. Car doors CRUMPED! shut.

Radio babble spun.

"There's the hat. Where's the cop?" a cop's reedy voice sounded.

"Yo! Inside the crowd."

More uniforms came into view.

"Get the blonde an ambulance," I wheezed.

"That's me?" Jody asked. "I'm 'the blonde?'"

It was no time for a debate on women's issues.

"Sorry, my love," I said. "Emergency cop-speak."

"That's another bad habit I have to break you from," she said.

She grimaced, rubbing her bloody mouth.

Mama Swifty gaped at us from outside Youth At Play. Her mouth hung open. She kept shaking her head.

"See that woman by the store?" I said. "Get precinct gold shields talking to her about Junior here. She'll have lots to say."

"We might as well send for the bus," another cop said. "Pack it full of cops."

"I need an ambulance," Lila said. "I might have to sue somebody about my back pain."

"My knee hurts, too," another said.

Eddie the beer-drinker groaned and rolled onto his belly.

"Jesus," he kept saying. "I hurt all over."

"This is a 10-13 Unusual," a ropy-poly man sergeant said. "The bosses were up here on these murders."

"And here they come now."

"Remember the fricking regulations. Everyone put their hats on."

Captain Day bellied into my view. He was sweating through his white boss's shirt.

"Royster, what have you got?" he asked.

"I thought you'd never ask," I said. "I'm arresting this Horn Bug, Junior Swifty or something, for double murder and Attempt Murder on me."

"For real?"

"How real do you want it?" I asked.

Lipkin and Hundshamer came up alongside Day. Hundshamer pinned his gold shield to his suit jacket lapel with his scarred hand shaking.

The uniforms yanked the Horn Bug off the sidewalk and into a car.

He glared and spat at me, missing.

"I'm back in Patrol again," I said. "I'm appreciated as usual."

Captain Day formed a harsh noise in his throat.

"Those are my cuffs on him, you wonderful hammerhead guys," I said. "So don't none of you try stealing my arrest."

"Don't sweat, pal. We don't have that much ambition."

"Not anymore," a uniform said.

"That ship has sailed," another agreed.

"Hey, Cap," I said, pushing it. "You know something? My beatniks just showed me that Community Policing works. I'm converted."

"That's because my plan worked," Day said. "Putting you out here, I mean."

I stared.

"Ambulances for these civilians!" Hundshamer shouted. "What's wrong with you uniforms?"

The roly-poly sergeant shook his head.

"Begging your pardon, CRIT Lieutenant, sir, but I did that getting out of my car," the sergeant said.

"You're going to claim that Max was following your orders?" Lipkin asked.

"Known only to a few in the Job," Day said.

"I bet," I said.

"Keep in mind, Captain," Lipkin said. "That I know the real deal. So forget about hurting Max. Ever."

Day looked around and made sure that Jody and the other beatniks were out of earshot. Cops listening to us smirked.

An ambulance screeched around the corner and stopped. Paramedics bloomed forth.

"Lt. Hundshamer," Lipkin said, "Is Max cleared?"

Hundshamer looked guilty about everything.

"I never charged him with anything," he said. "I always admired him."

"Aw, go eat your own hand," a uniform shouted from the shadows.

"CRIT rat," a supporter said.

"Actually, I overreacted," Day said. "I was grieving over my son and my judgment lapsed for a while. So I made this plan. That led me to accuse Royster and build his cover so I could use him as my undercover officer."

"Really?" I said.

"There were never any real charges against him," Day said. "I'm at peace with everything. Now that I'm operating with a clear head, I can speak to the media about the plan that Max and I had worked out."

I blew out a breath and sagged. Blood dripped from my elbow and face. My smashed lips swelled. I would need stitches again.

"Good idea," I said. "Captain Day, your plan to put me here undercover in uniform was brilliant."

"I may throw up," Lipkin said.

"But do it before the media shows up," I said. "We have to quash those fake charges that had everyone fooled."

"You can't pull that off," Hundshamer said.

"Watch us," I said, brushing Day's chin with my fist, boxer-fashion. "Cap Day and I are a team."

Day choked but he managed a grin.

"Of course there's no charges on Max," Jody said, limping over. "Because I'm going to take him home and love him forever."

Special thanks once again to:

To Persia Walker, novelist, for her untiring help and suggestions.

To Detective-Investigators Mark Baldessare and Fareed "Fred" Ghussin and all the other cops and federal agents who taught me so much about hunting our real-life serial killers.

To the ***Spy, the Movie*** team – Jim MacPherson, Alex Klymko, Charles Messina and all the rest of the gang for a grand adventure in screenwriting.

To Nad Wolinska for her as always inventive cover illustration and Richard Amari for his equally inventive cover design.

To my writing partner, Lynwood Shiva Sawyer, for his support and encouragement over the years

And my thanks to that wonderful woman, companion and friend from Guangzhou, China, who shares my adventures and my life.

If you enjoyed ***Funny Bunny Hunts the Horn Bug***, you might like to read what other readers wrote about Frank Hickey's previous Max Royster novel, ***The Gypsy Twist.***

ଓ

"I got so interested in the book that I finished it in one night! I simply could not stop reading. I am eagerly awaiting his next book."

~ **Ray Beauchesne** (90-year-old World War II veteran, South Pacific Theater)

"When my husband and I were on our honeymoon, I brought along ***The Gypsy Twist*** and. started reading it The story carried me away. My husband got curious and took over the book. He read the first four chapters and said, 'This is an interesting book.'"

~ **Wan Hsiu Lan** (International concert pianist from Taiwan)

"I liked the characters in ***The Gypsy Twist***, their definitions, their interactions, their loyalties and conflicts. The plot is genuine. So is the police work, the experience – the frustrations and methods they use and WON'T use to do theirs work."

~ **Marcus Lavieri** (Actor, musician and one of the last shepherds left in the state of Connecticut)

"Mr. Hickey's fast-paced opening pages resonated with this New Yorker's alarming experience of being violently ambushed beside the Central Park Reservoir one dusky Sunday afternoon. We residents can be thankful that Max Royster is courageously and intelligently on the job and will continue to be in future volumes."

~ **S.W.** (Name withheld by request, an Upper East Side crime victim)

"I'm not normally a fan of mysteries, but Frank Hickey's assured, confident voice could make me a convert (or at least to his work). He knows his way both around the genre, and the world of detectives, suspects, low-lifes and hard-boiled reporters. The result is a compelling page-turner about the ultimate scary teacher revenge."

~ **Merri Rosenberg** (*Education Update Online*)

The next Max Royster story is coming soon!

It's Christmas in Manhattan.

A blizzard whips the city.

The Beautiful People in the elite Upper East Side celebrate in their brownstones.

Until a kidnapper seizes a lovely young debutante.

Max Royster, fired from the NYPD for mental illness, fights the kidnapper but loses.

The kidnapper flees.

Stripped of gun, shield and power, Max has only his wits to save the victim.

The FBI treats Max like a suspect and tramples roughshod on his rights.

During this long sleepless night, an unknown FBI agent cracks up. Over the radio, he quotes J. Edgar Hoover and plants false clues .

To solve the case, Max must smash through the facade and mysteries of millionaires in their snug brownstones. Exotic women tempt him to give up.

The blizzard worsens.

As the winds howl and snowdrifts deepen, Max risks his life and his freedom in a desperate bid to save the victim.

Once again, Max Royster is back on the street in ***Brownstone Kidnap Crackup***.